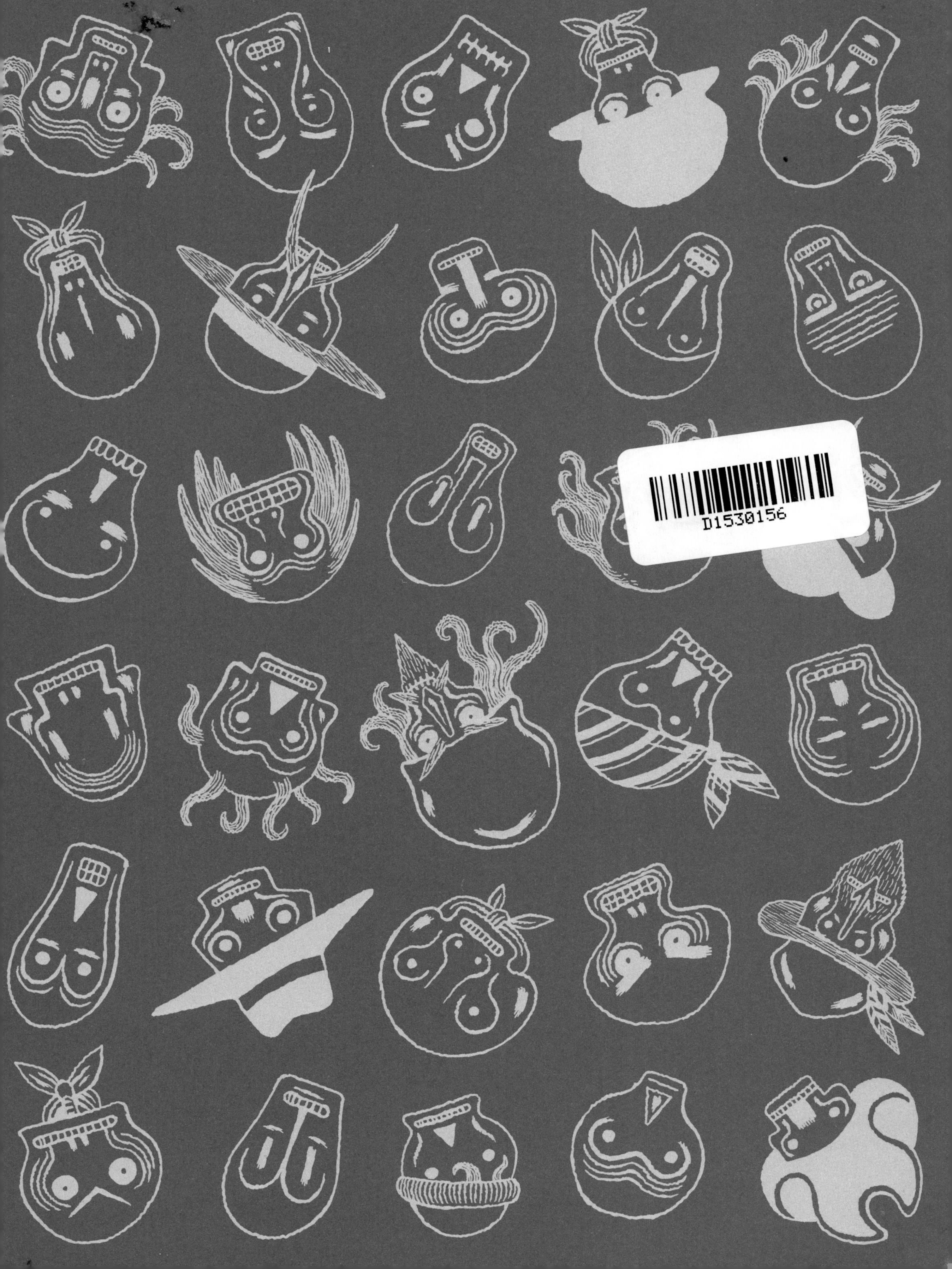

DAVID B. & PIERRE MAC ORLAN

The Littlest Pirate King

FANTAGRAPHICS BOOKS

Other books by David B. available in English:
The Armed Garden (Fantagraphics Books, coming in 2011)
Babel #1 (Drawn and Quarterly)
Babel #2 (Fantagraphics Books)
Babel #3 (Fantagraphics Books, coming in 2011)
Epileptic (Pantheon)
Nocturnal Conspiracies (NBM)

Edited and translated by Kim Thompson. Book design by Jacob Covey. Production by Paul Baresh. Lettering by Alexa Koenings. Title lettering by Céline Merrien. Associate Editor: Eric Reynolds. Published by Gary Groth and Kim Thompson. *The Littlest Pirate King (Le Roi rose)* © 2009 Gallimard Jeunesse. This edition © 2010 Fantagraphics Books. All rights reserved, permission to quote or reproduce material for reviews or notices must be obtained from Fantagraphics Books, in writing, at 7563 Lake City Way NE, Seattle, WA 98115. Visit Fantagraphics online at www.fantagraphics.com. Distributed to bookstores in the U.S. by W.W. Norton and Company, Inc. (212-354-5500). Distributed to comics shops in the U.S. by Diamond Comic Distributors (800-452-6642). Distributed in Canada by Canadian Manda Group (416-516-0911). First edition September, 2010. Printed in Singapore ISBN 978-1-60699-403-0.

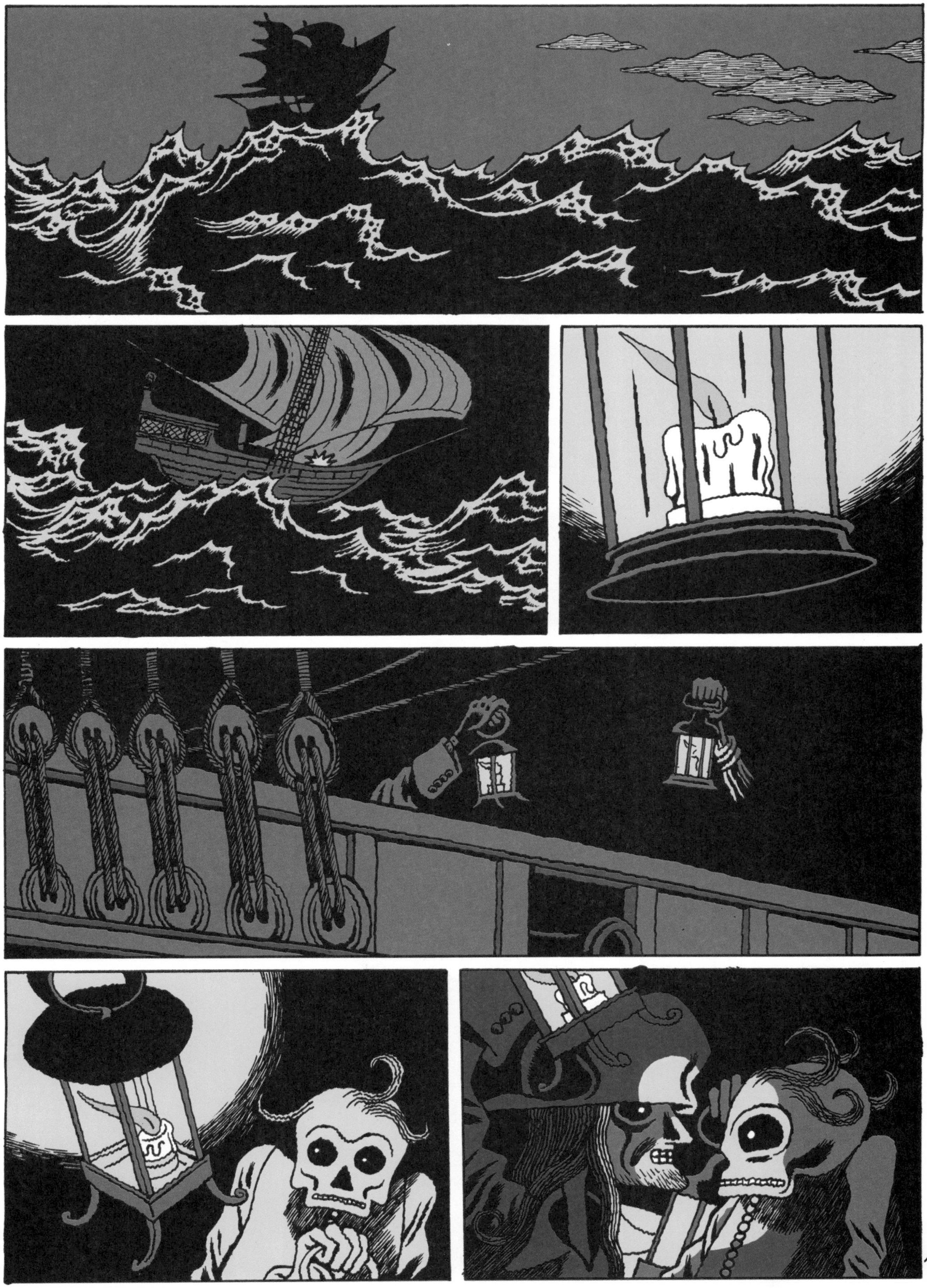

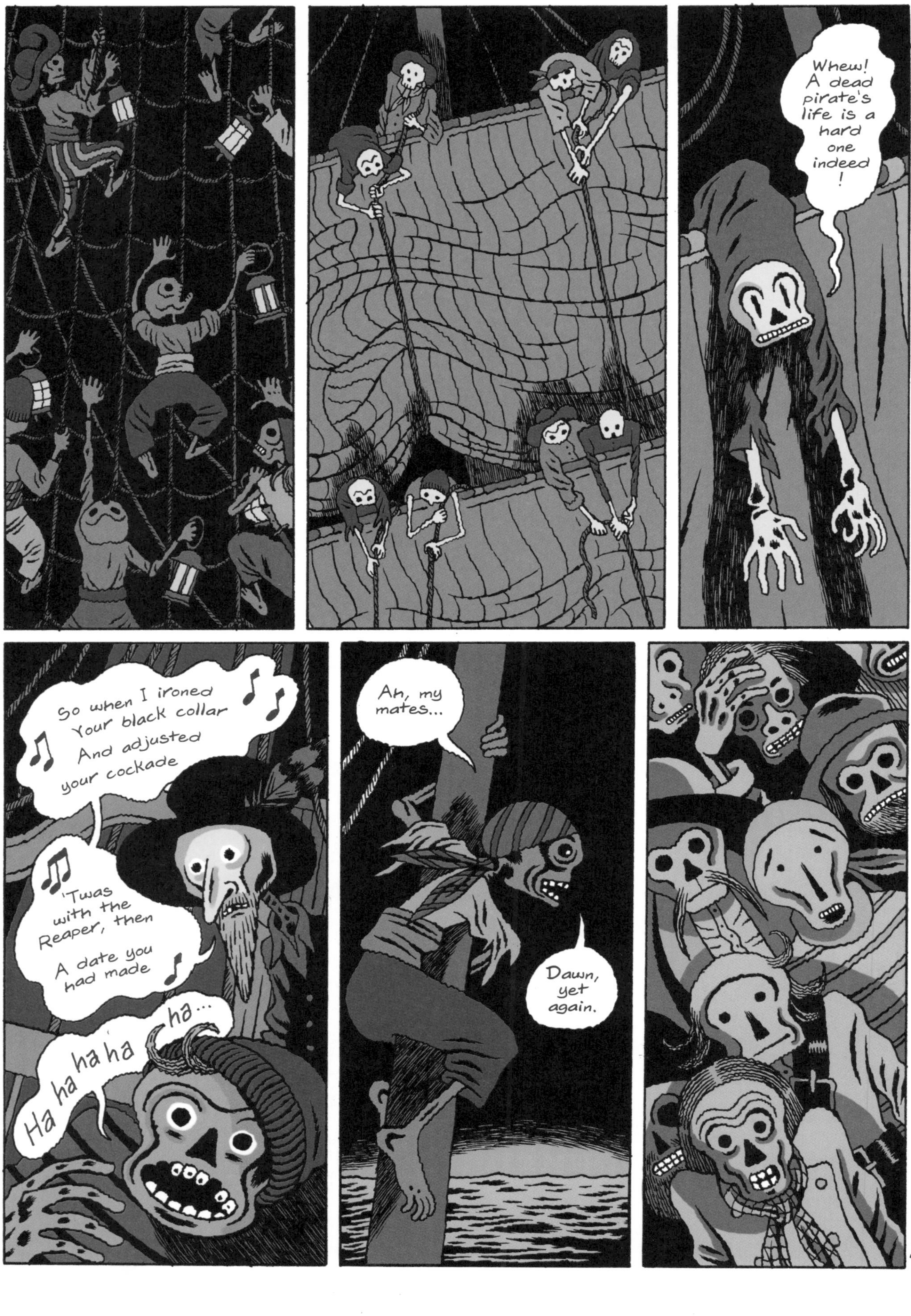
Whew! A dead pirate's life is a hard one indeed !
So when I ironed Your black collar And adjusted your cockade
'Twas with the Reaper, then A date you had made
Ha ha ha ha ha...
Ah, my mates...
Dawn, yet again.

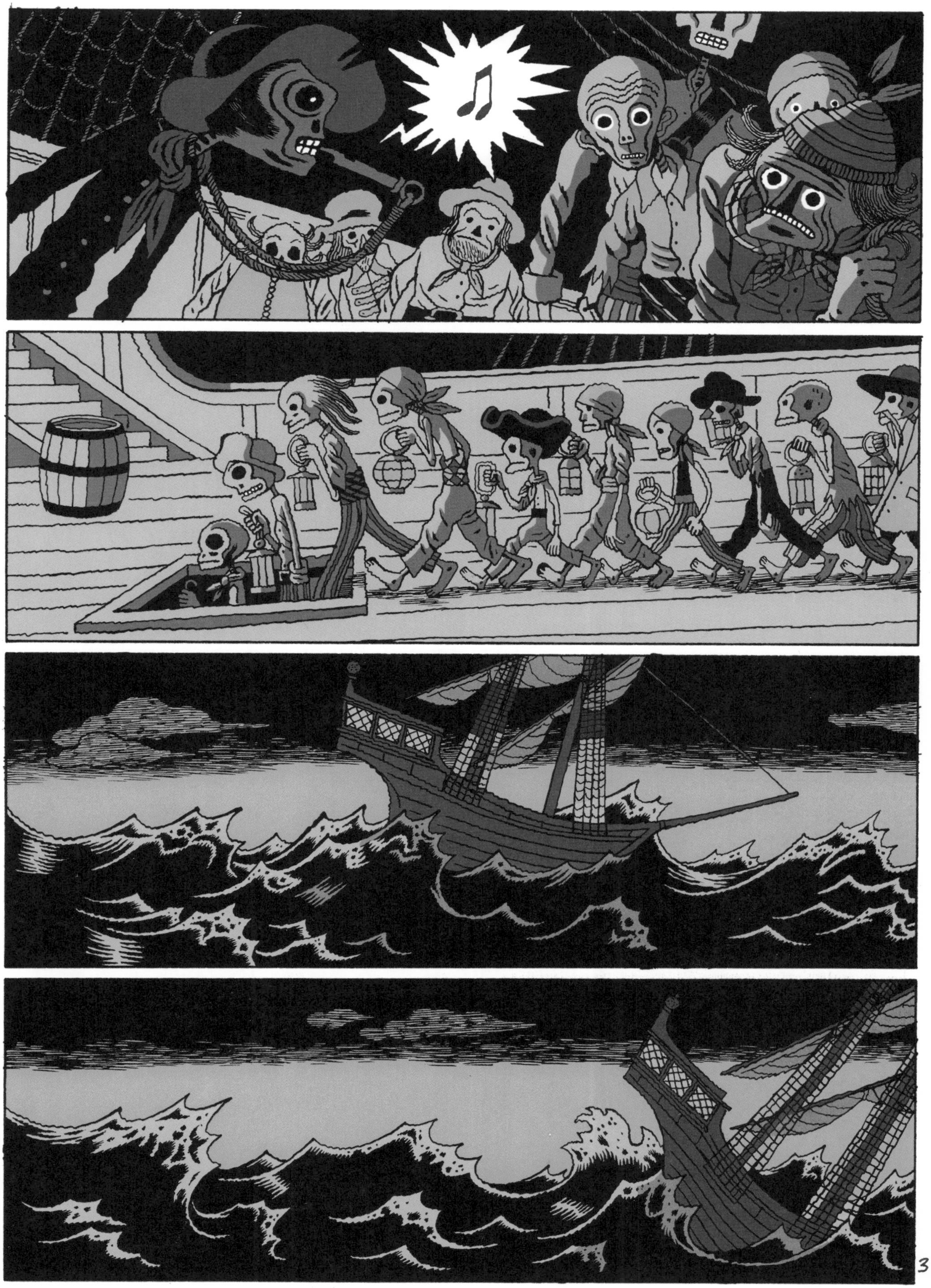

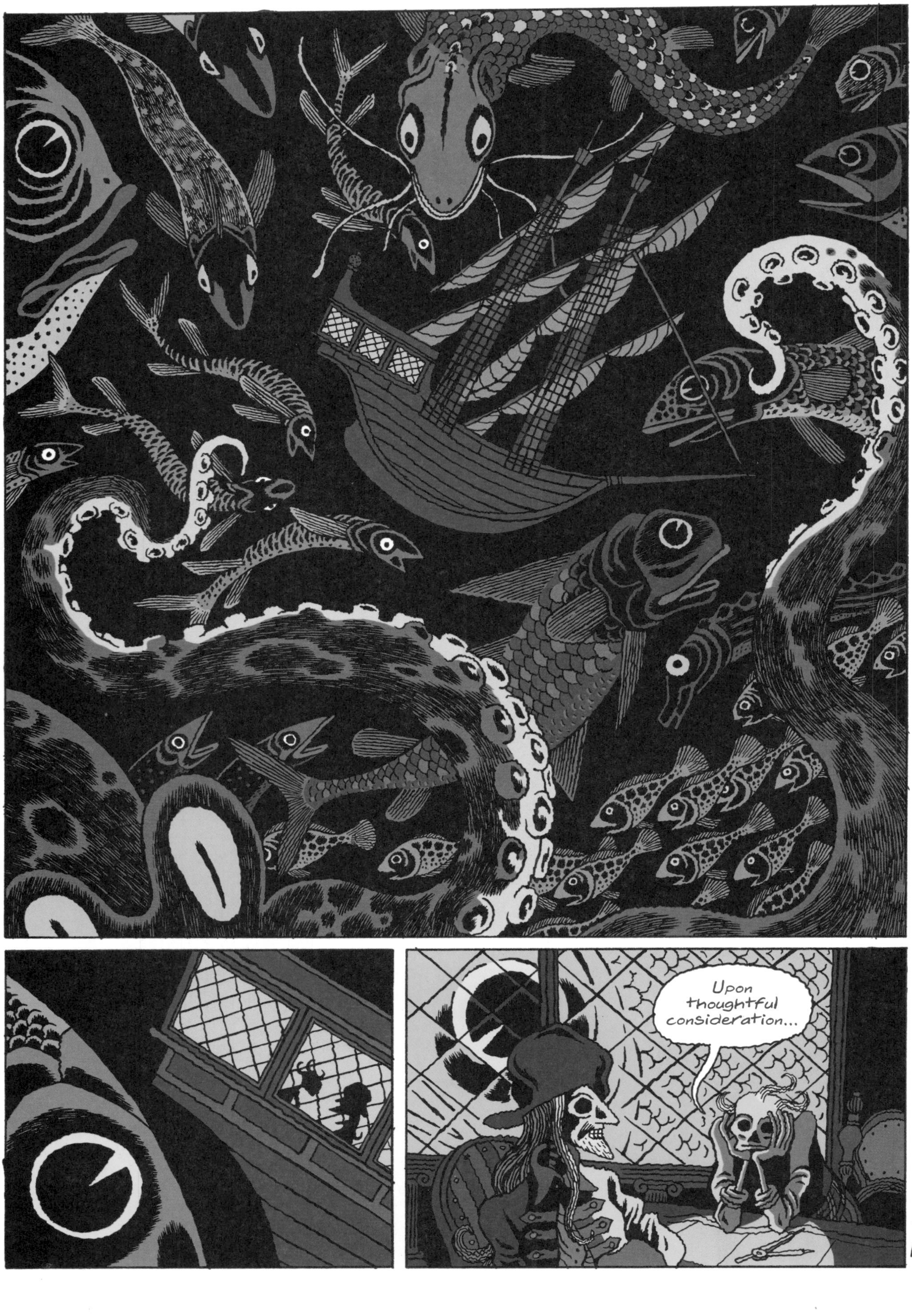
Upon thoughtful consideration...

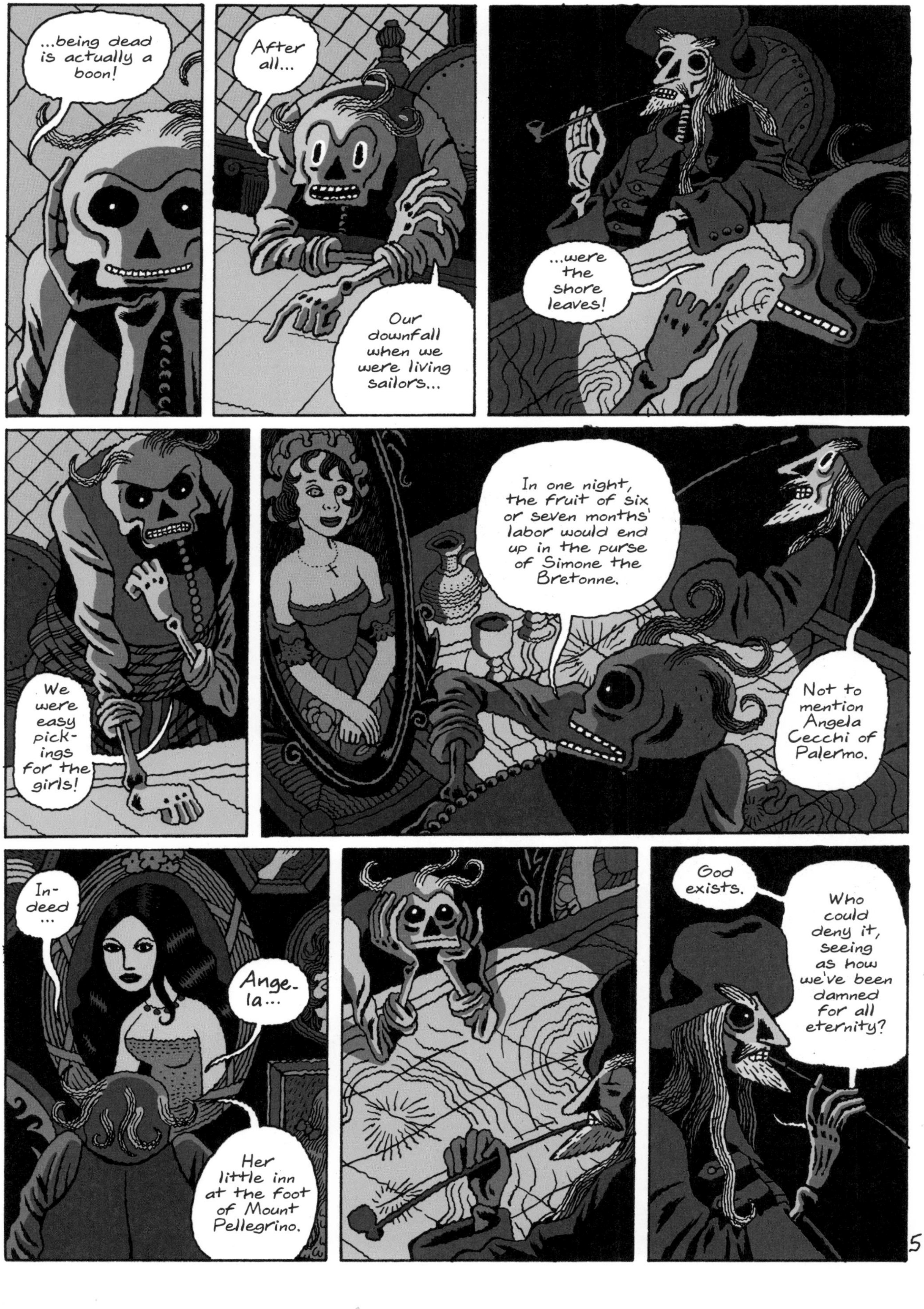
...being dead is actually a boon!
After all...
Our downfall when we were living sailors...
...were the shore leaves!
We were easy pick-ings for the girls!
In one night, the fruit of six or seven months' labor would end up in the purse of Simone the Bretonne.
Not to mention Angela Cecchi of Palermo.
In-deed...
Ange-la...
Her little inn at the foot of Mount Pellegrino.
God exists.
Who could deny it, seeing as how we've been damned for all eternity?

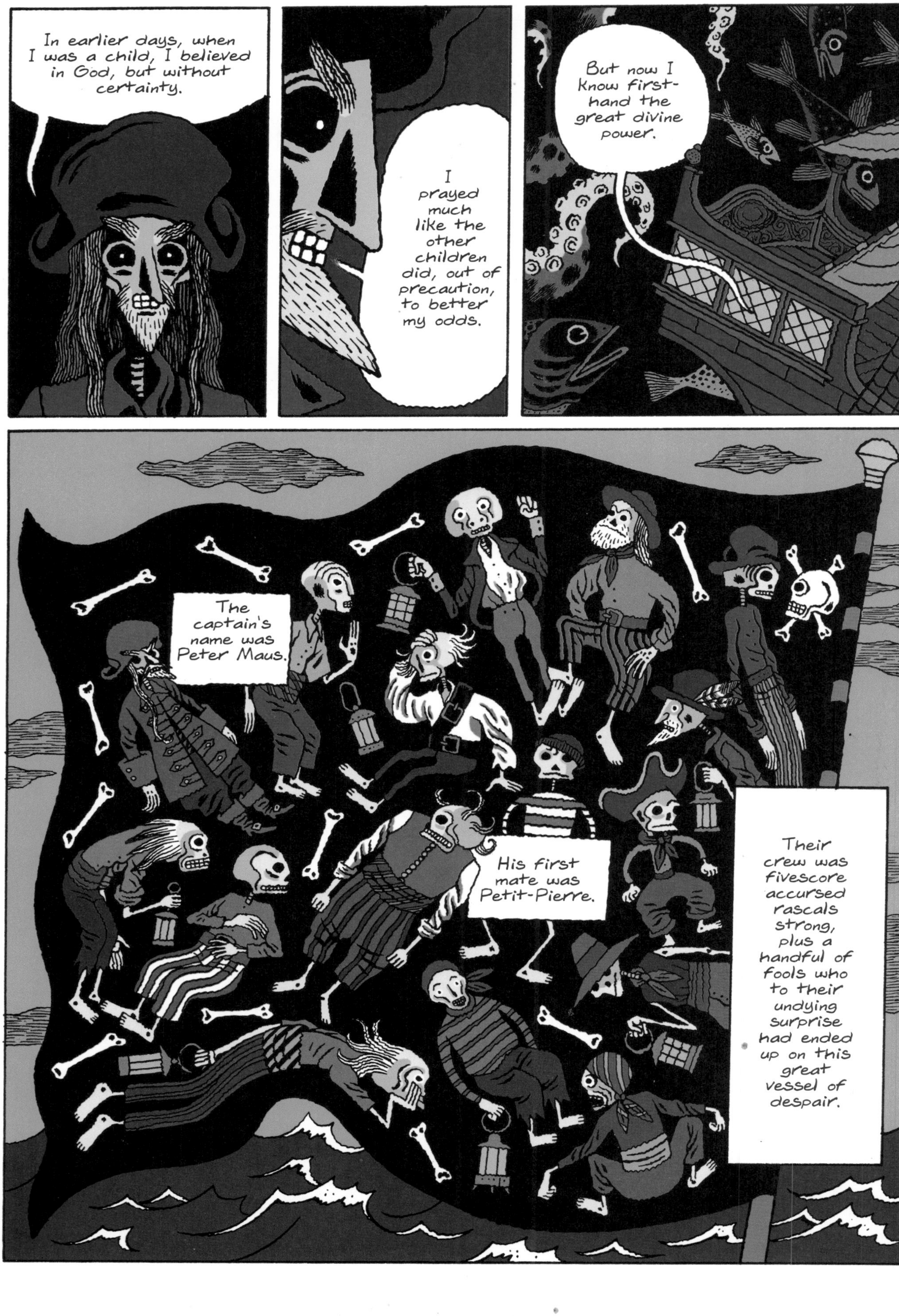

In earlier days, when I was a child, I believed in God, but without certainty.
I prayed much like the other children did, out of precaution, to better my odds.
But now I know first-hand the great divine power.
The captain's name was Peter Maus.
His first mate was Petit-Pierre.
Their crew was fivescore accursed rascals strong, plus a handful of fools who to their undying surprise had ended up on this great vessel of despair.

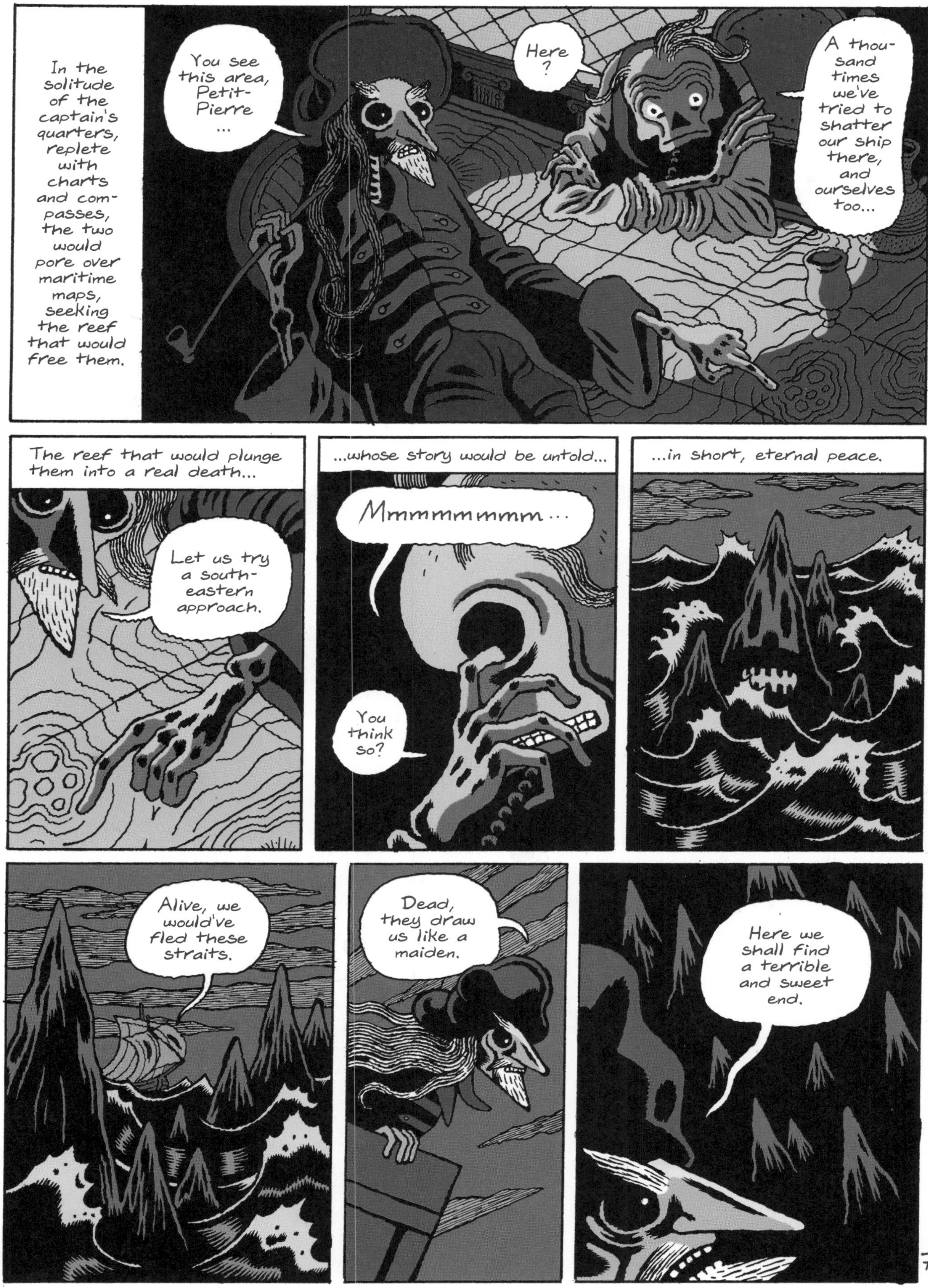
In the solitude of the captain's quarters, replete with charts and compasses, the two would pore over maritime maps, seeking the reef that would free them.
You see this area, Petit-Pierre ...
Here ?
A thousand times we've tried to shatter our ship there, and ourselves too...
The reef that would plunge them into a real death...
Let us try a south-eastern approach.
...whose story would be untold...
Mmmmmmmmm...
You think so?
...in short, eternal peace.
Alive, we would've fled these straits.
Dead, they draw us like a maiden.
Here we shall find a terrible and sweet end.

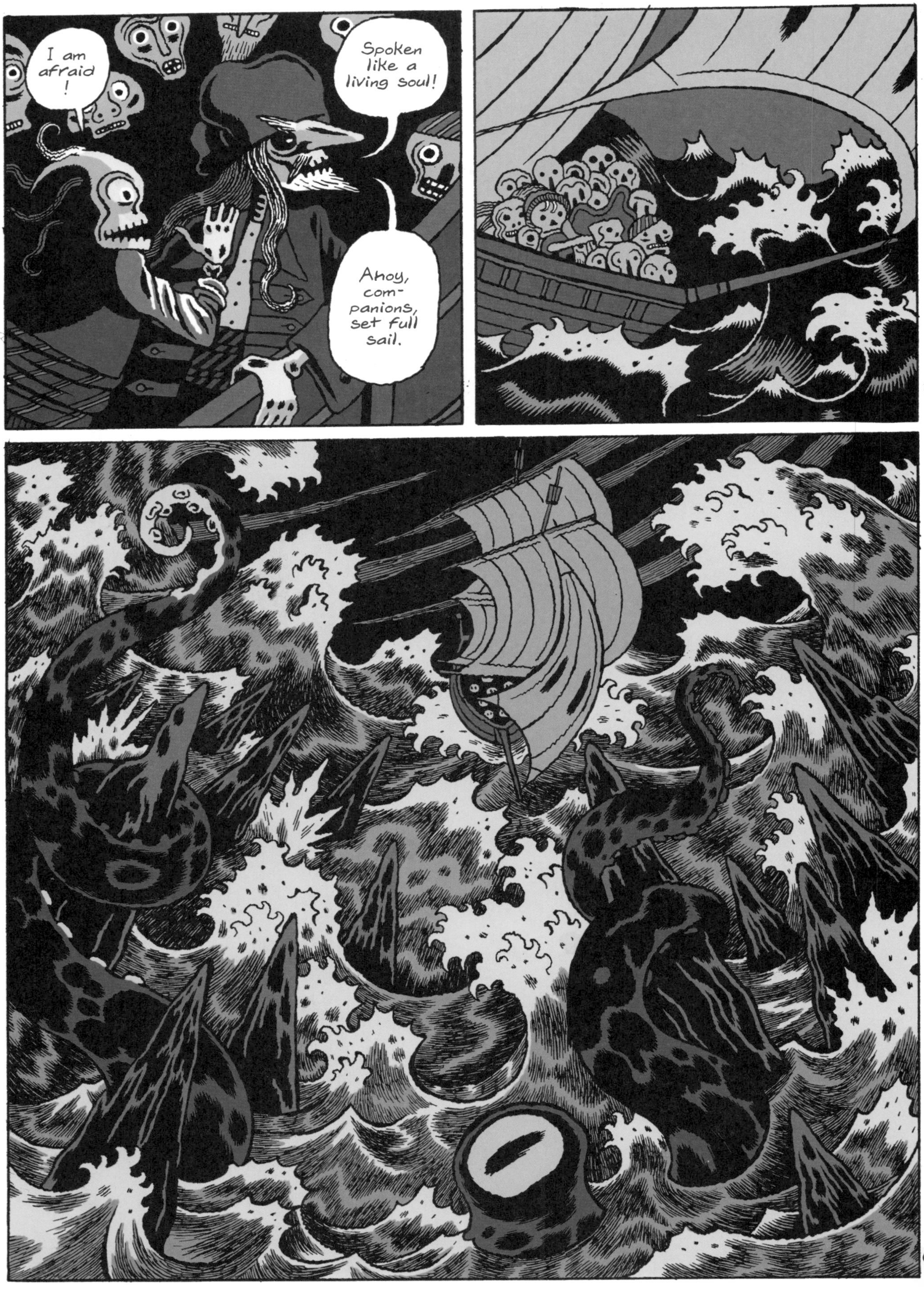
I am afraid!
Spoken like a living soul!
Ahoy, companions, set full sail.

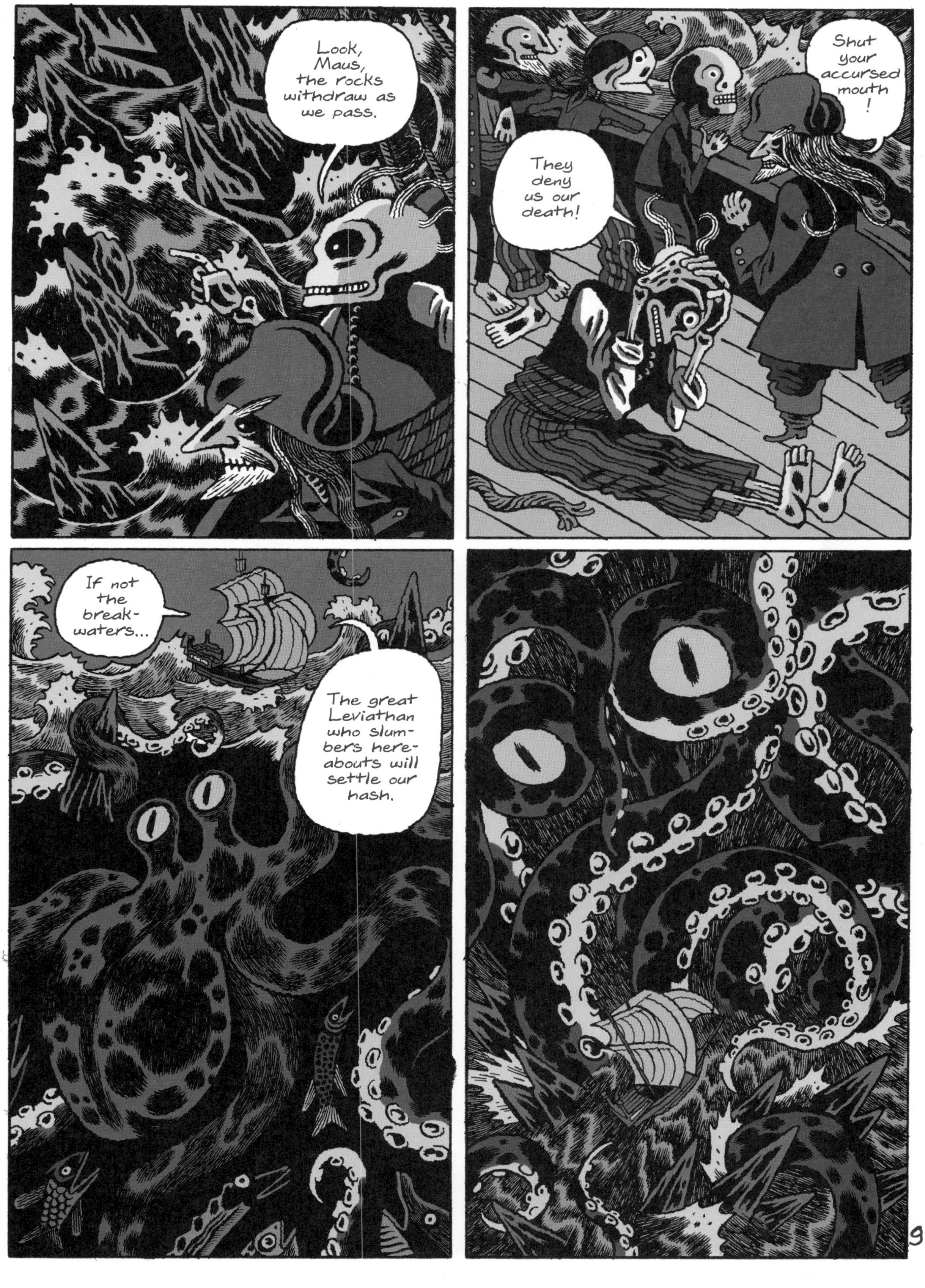
Look, Maus, the rocks withdraw as we pass.
Shut your accursed mouth !
They deny us our death!
If not the breakwaters...
The great Leviathan who slumbers hereabouts will settle our hash.

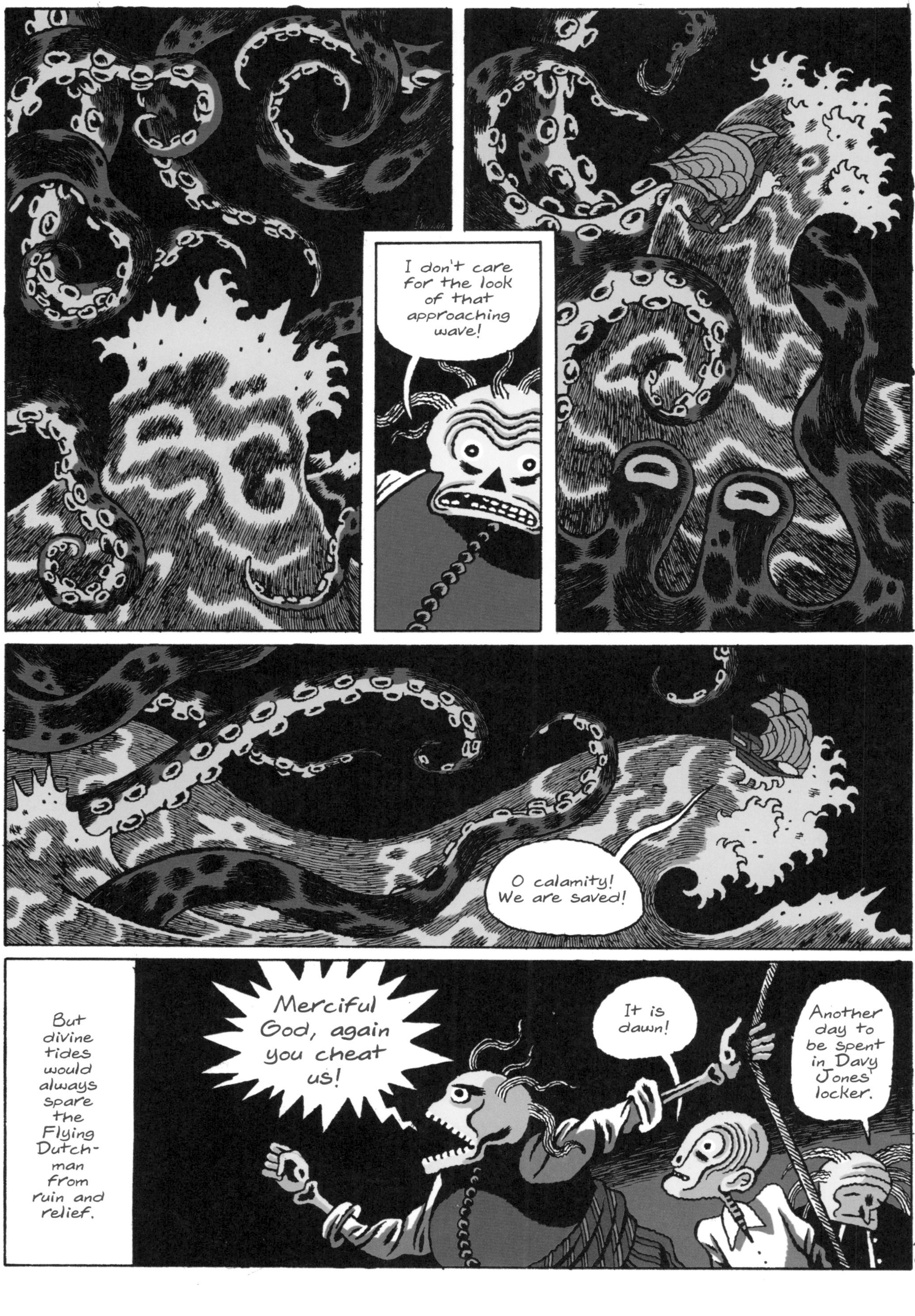

I don't care for the look of that approaching wave!
O calamity! We are saved!
But divine tides would always spare the Flying Dutch-man from ruin and relief.
Merciful God, again you cheat us!
It is dawn!
Another day to be spent in Davy Jones' locker.

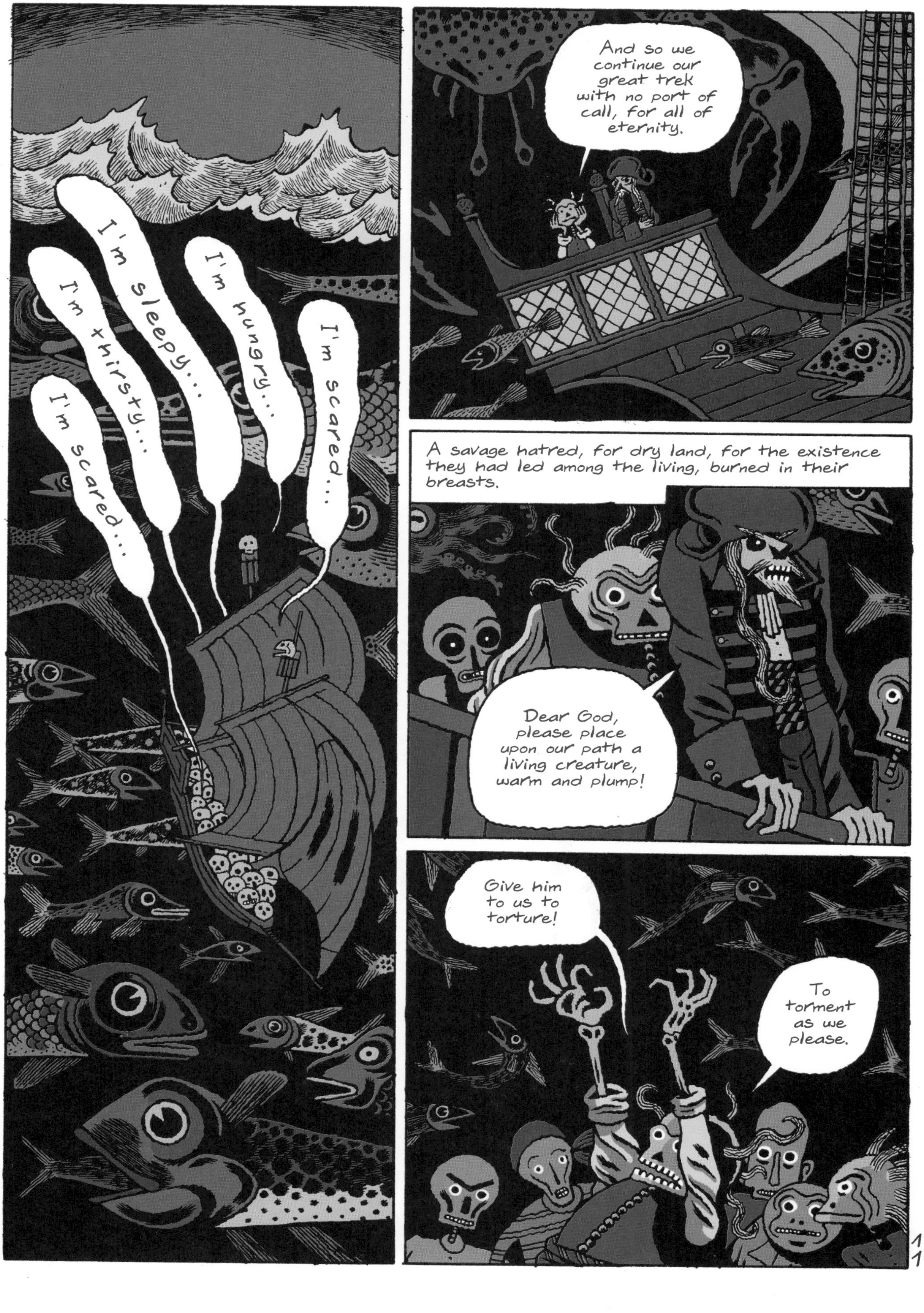
I'm scared...
I'm thirsty...
I'm sleepy...
I'm hungry...
I'm scared...
And so we continue our great trek with no port of call, for all of eternity.
A savage hatred, for dry land, for the existence they had led among the living, burned in their breasts.
Dear God, please place upon our path a living creature, warm and plump!
Give him to us to torture!
To torment as we please.

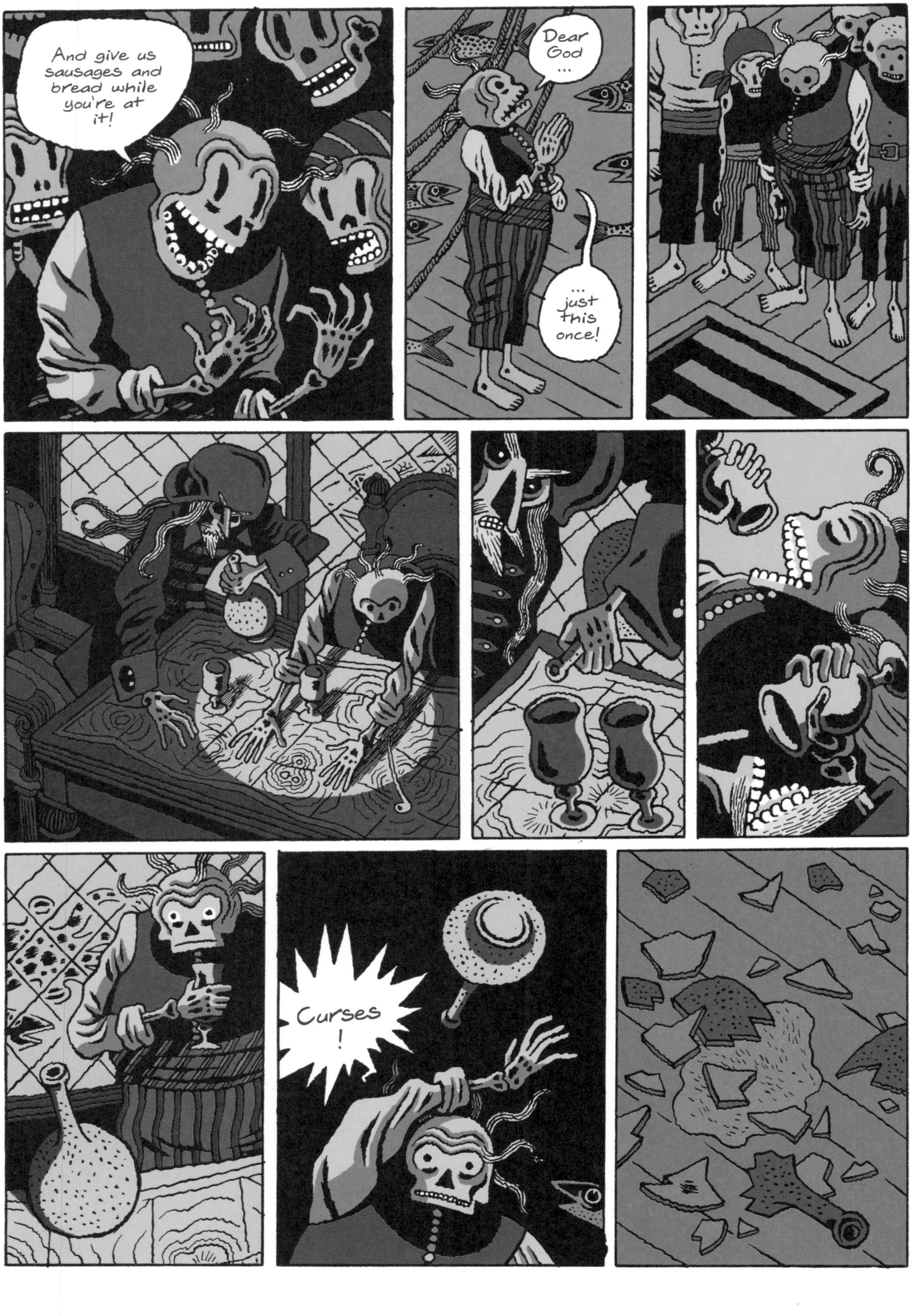
And give us sausages and bread while you're at it!
Dear God ...
... just this once!
Curses !

Don't break that damn'd bottle, or we shan't be able to pretend to drink!
fff...
Petit-Pierre to the bridge, night is breaking!
Should we come across a vessel of the living, we shall make them pay dearly for the curse that weighs upon us!
Then our dam-nation will be deeper yet.
So what !

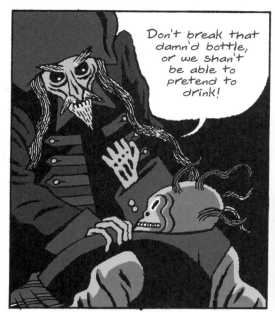

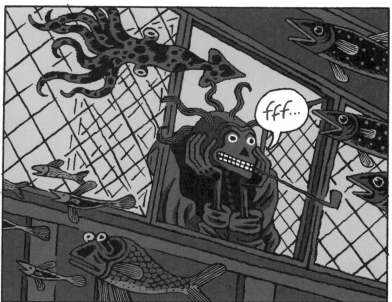

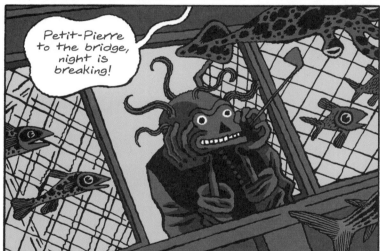

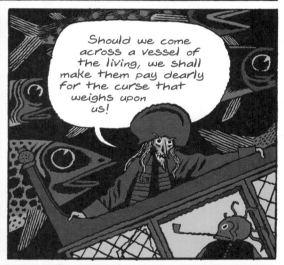

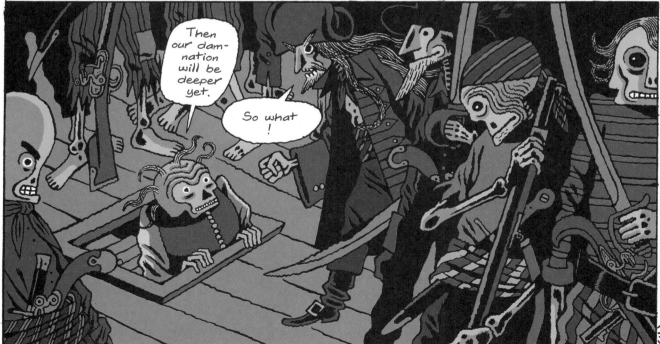

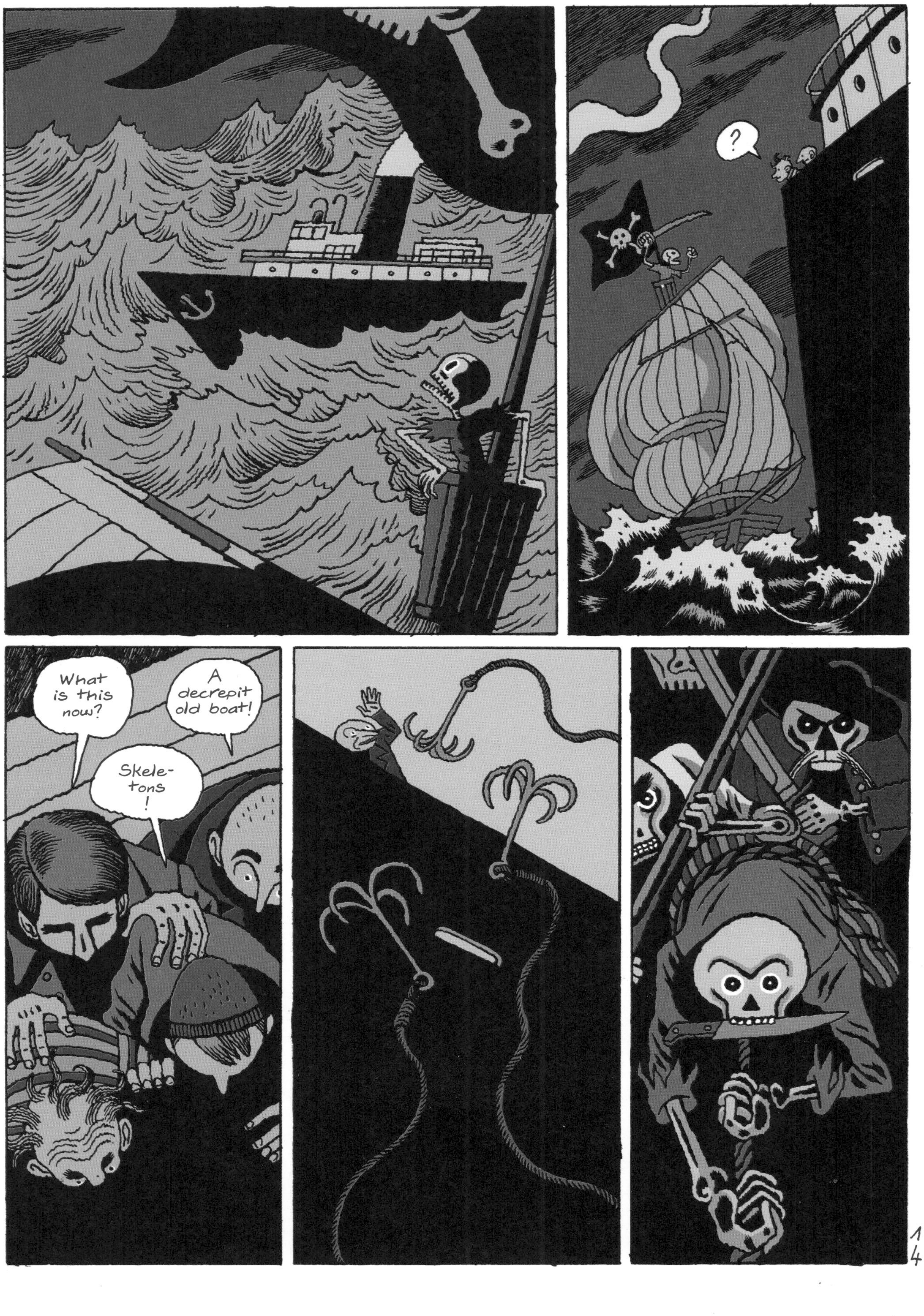
?
What is this now?
A decrepit old boat!
Skeletons!

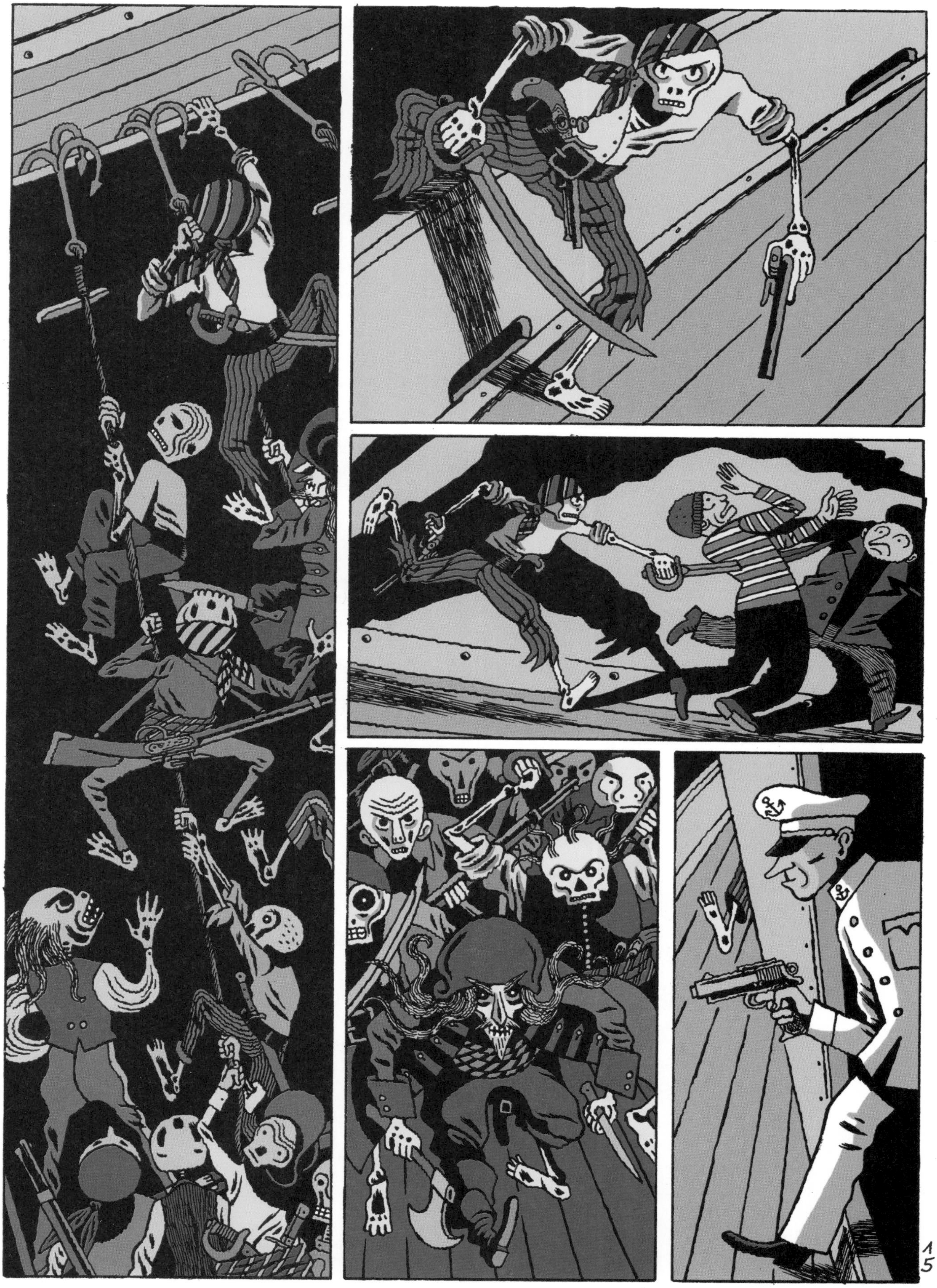

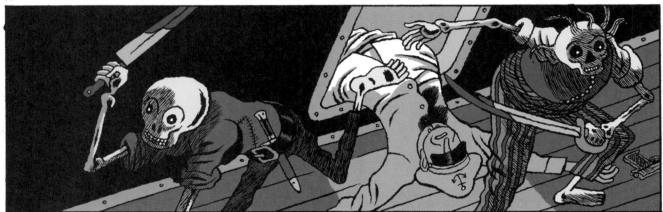

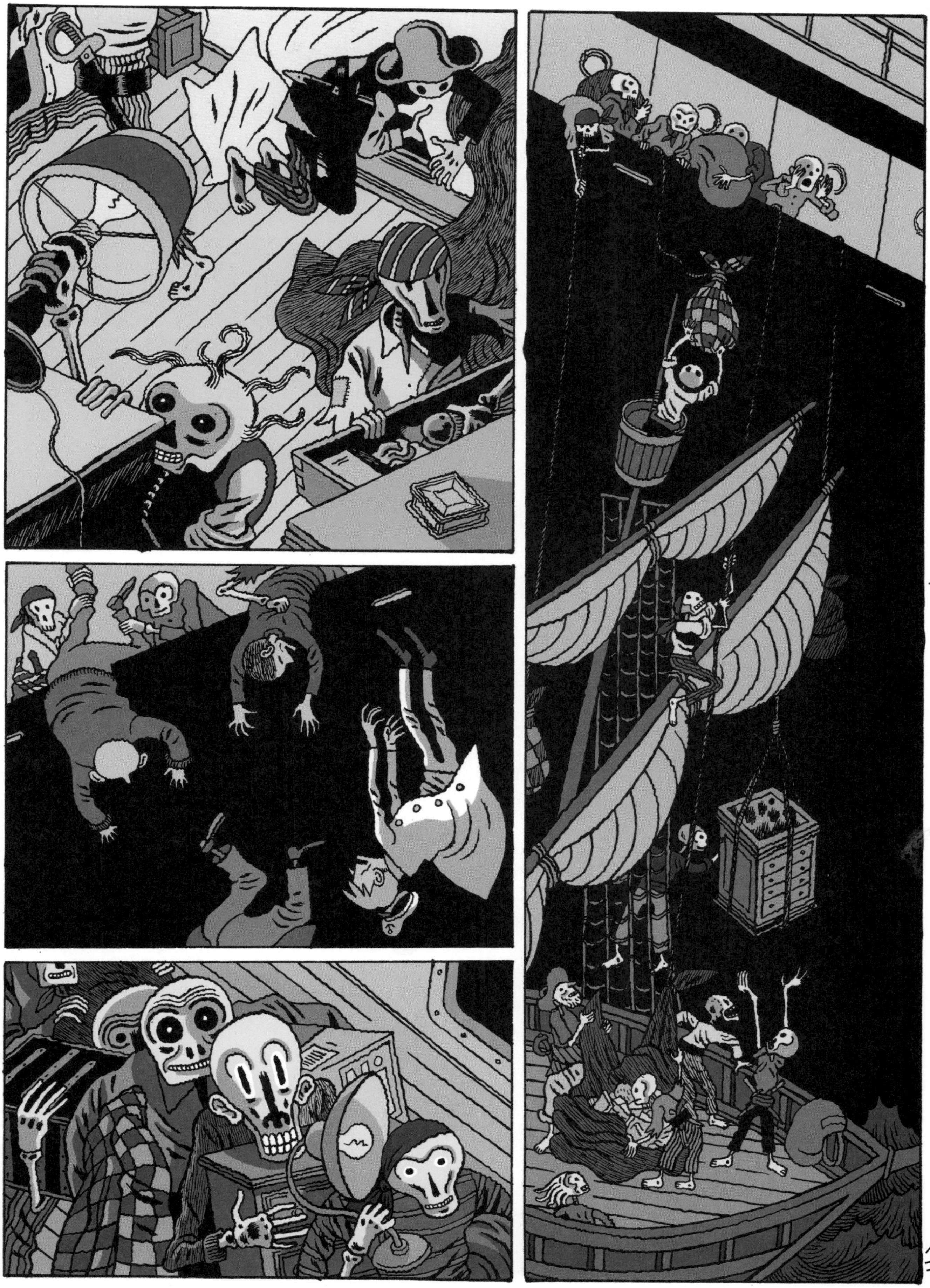

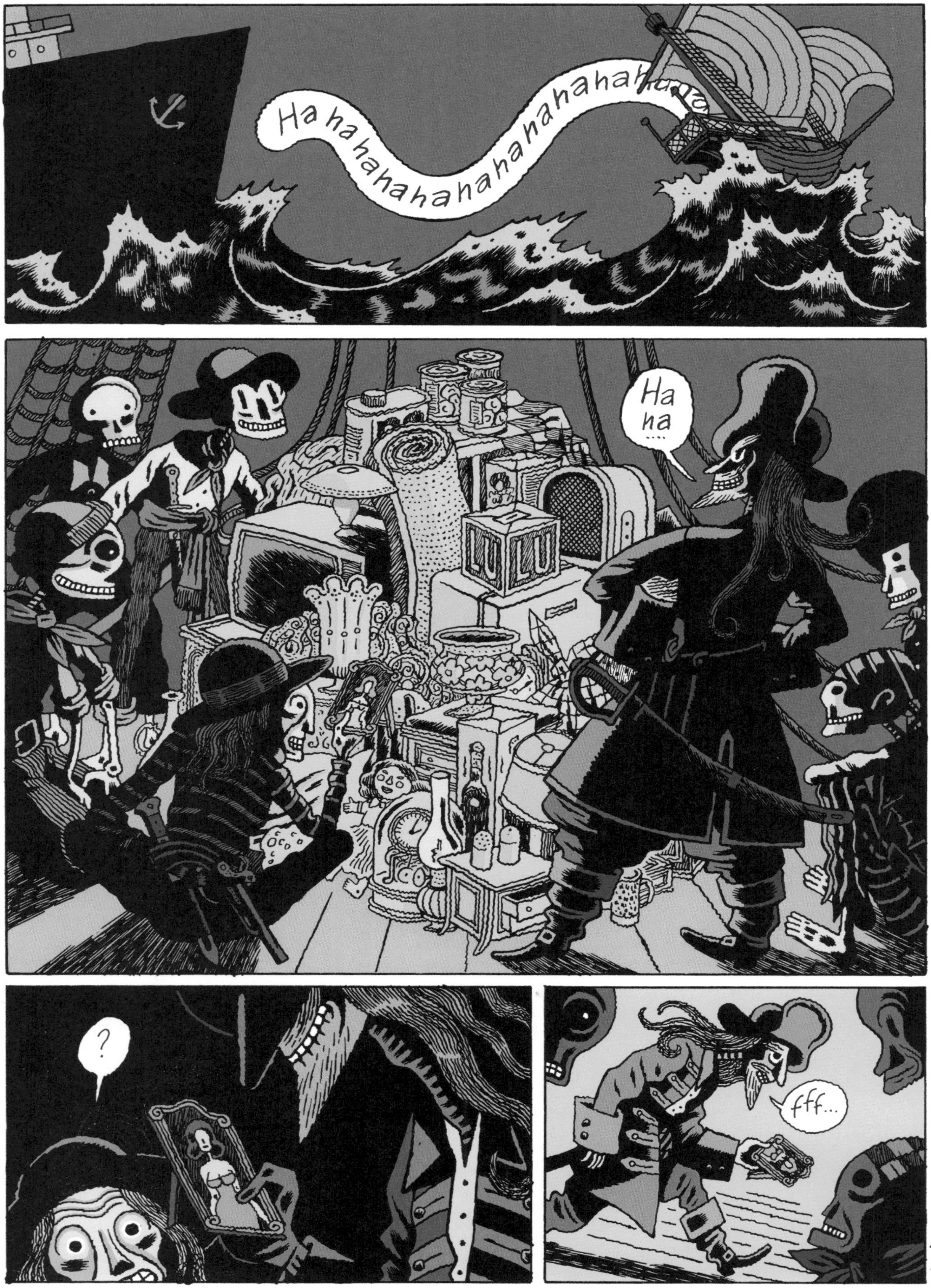
Ha ha hahahahahahahahahahaha
Ha ha ....
?
fff...

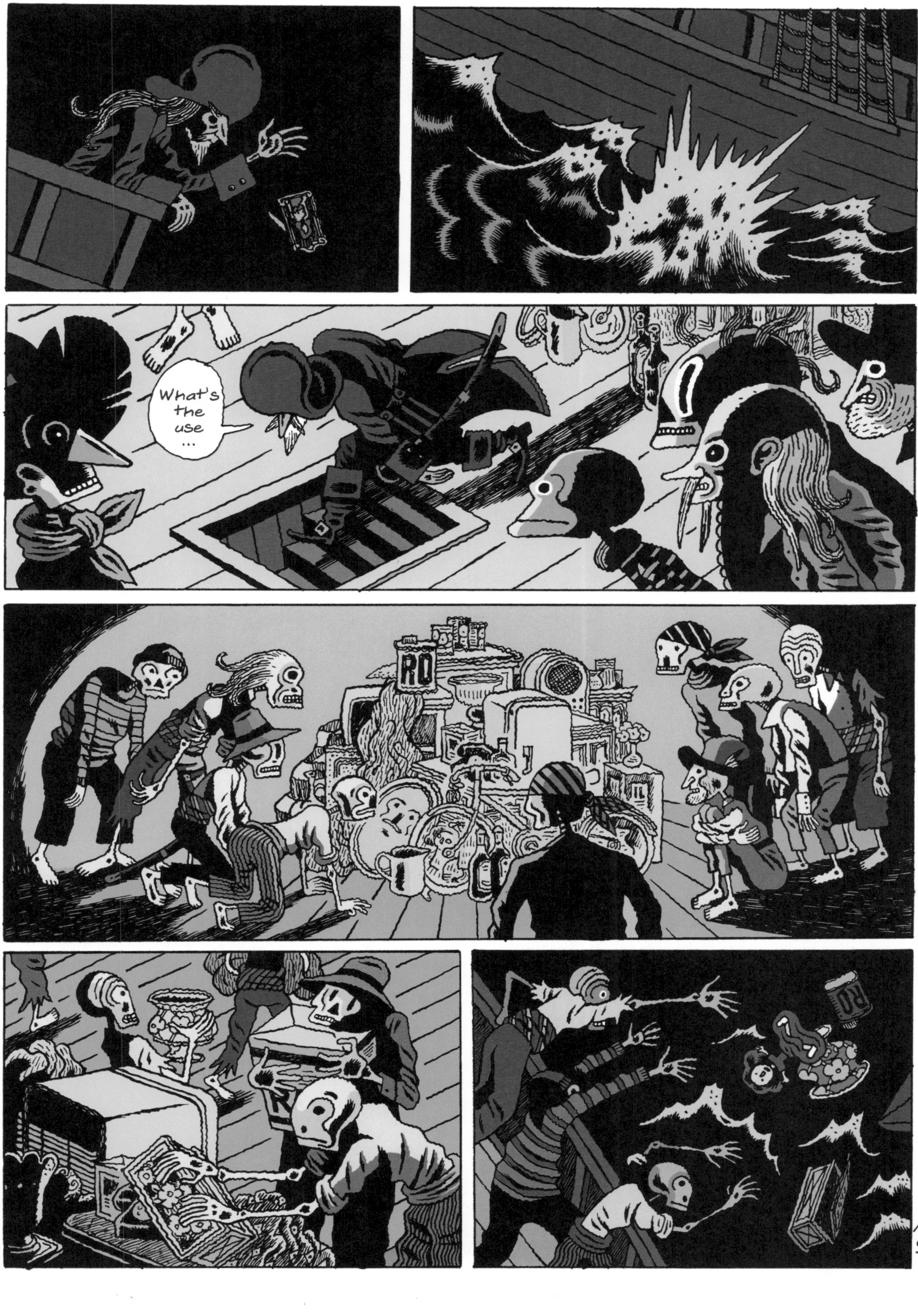
What's the use ...

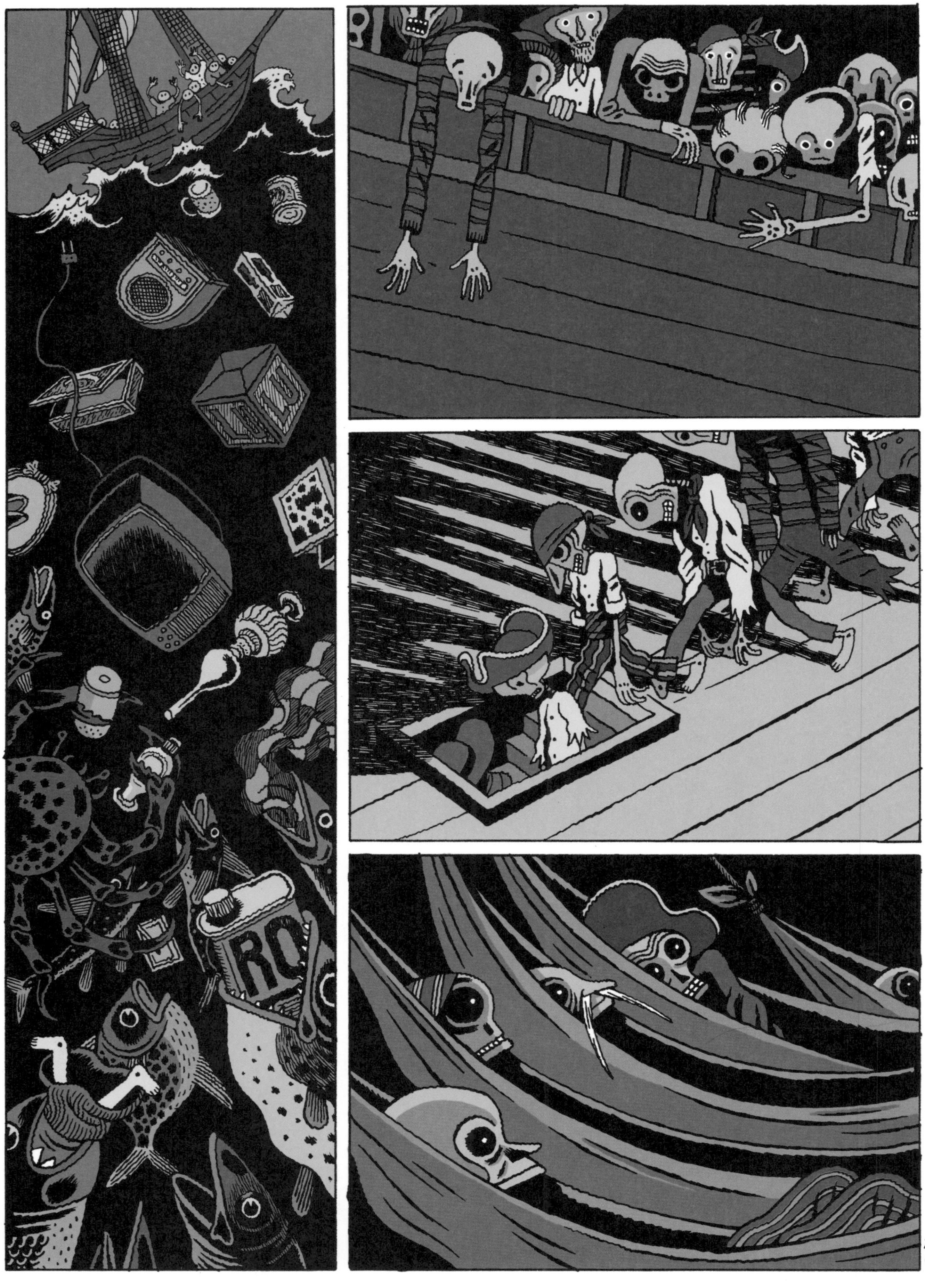

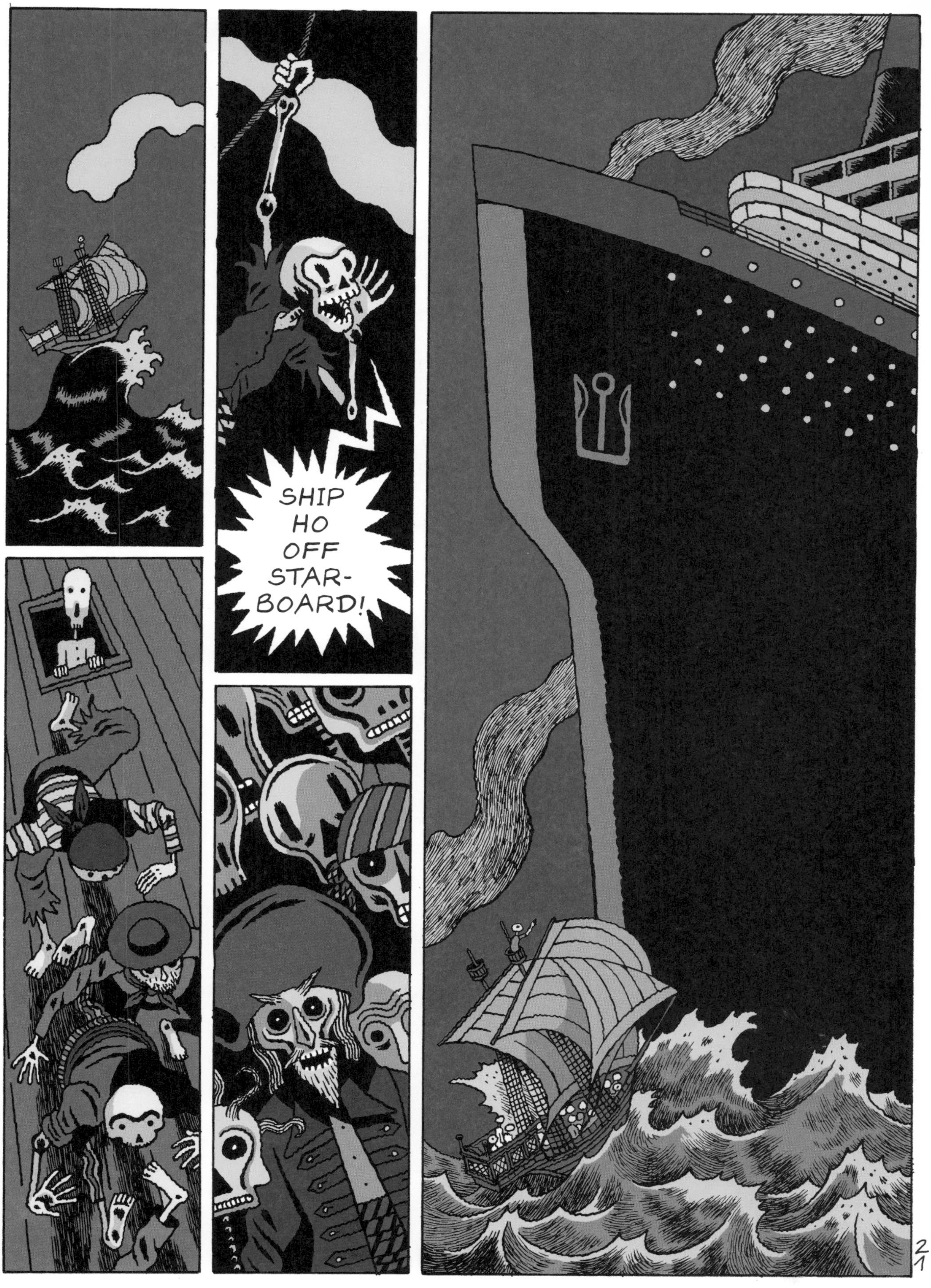
SHIP HO OFF STAR-BOARD!

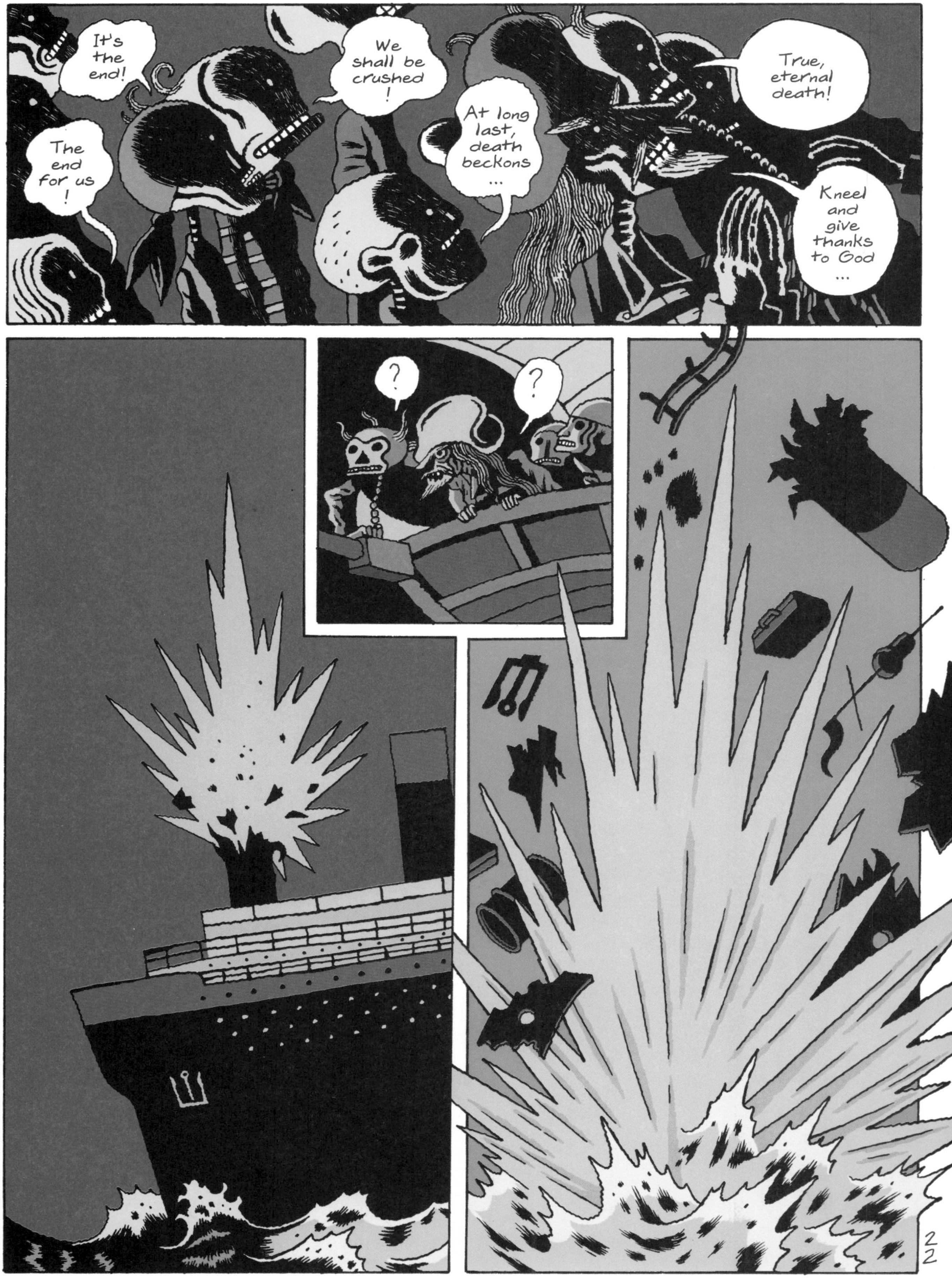
It's the end!
The end for us !
We shall be crushed !
At long last, death beckons ...
True, eternal death!
Kneel and give thanks to God ...
?
?

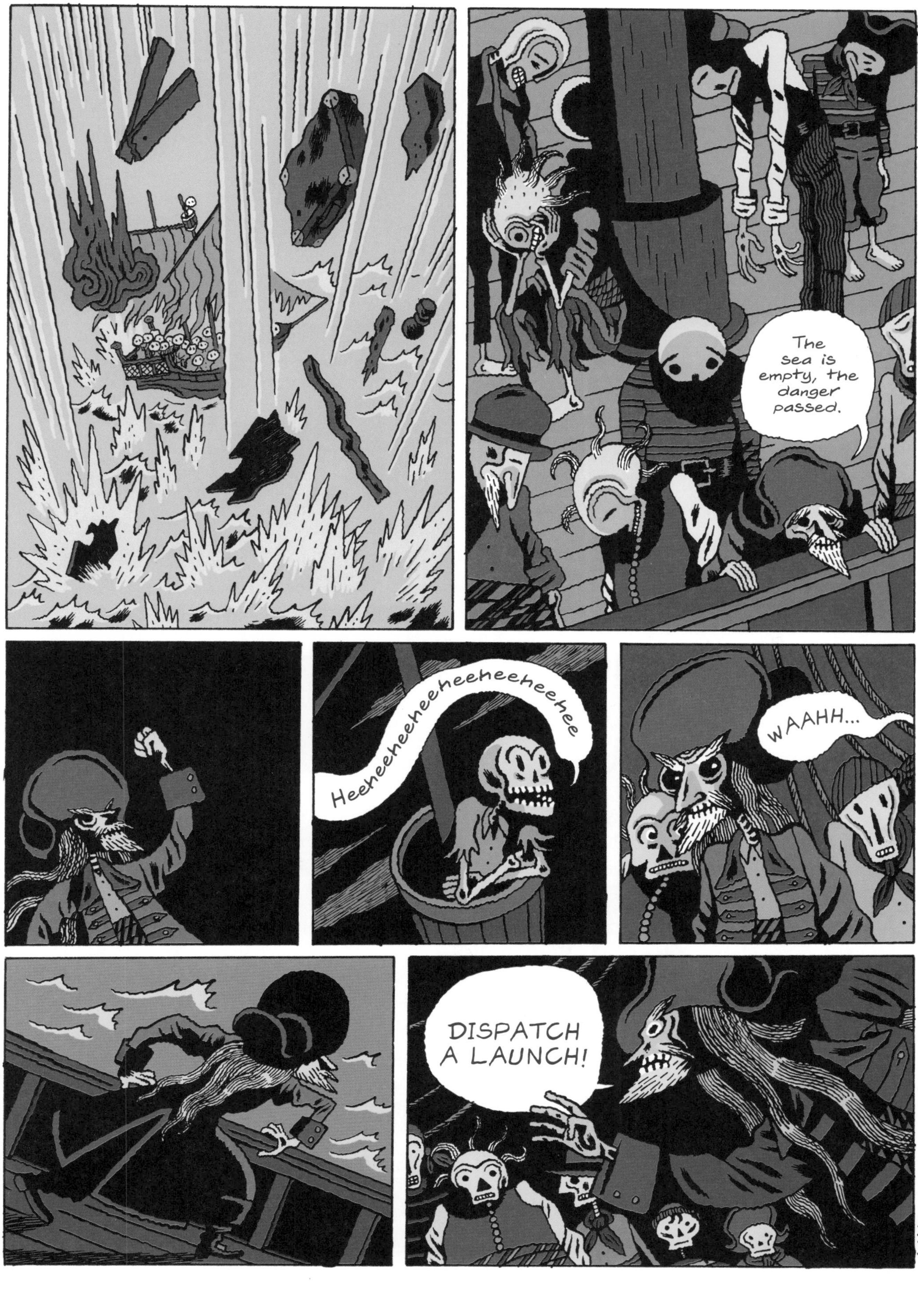

The sea is empty, the danger passed.
Heeheeheeheeheeheeheeheehee
WAAHH...
DISPATCH A LAUNCH!

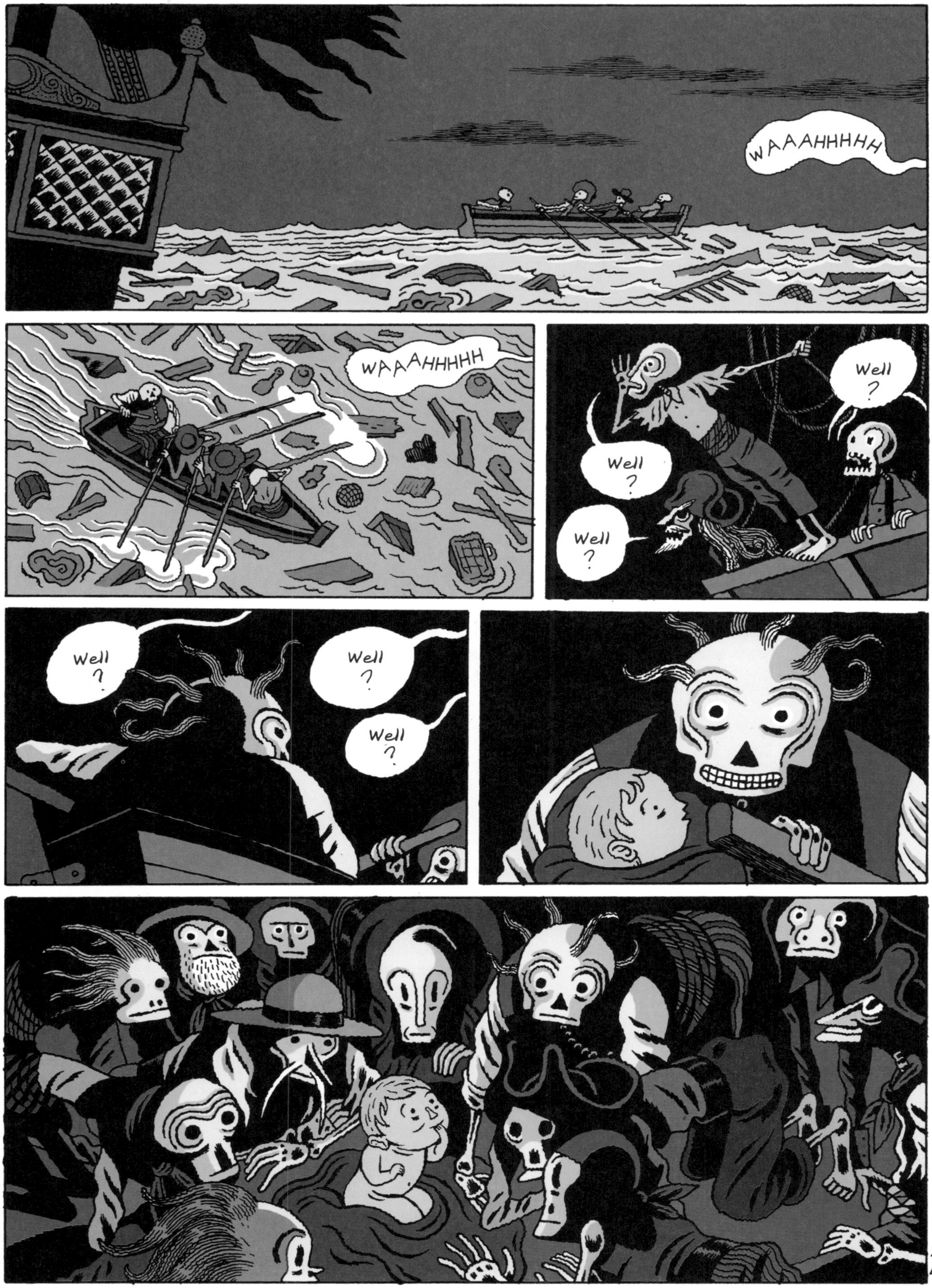
WAAAHHHHH
WAAAHHHHH
Well ?
Well ?
Well ?
Well ?
Well ?
Well ?

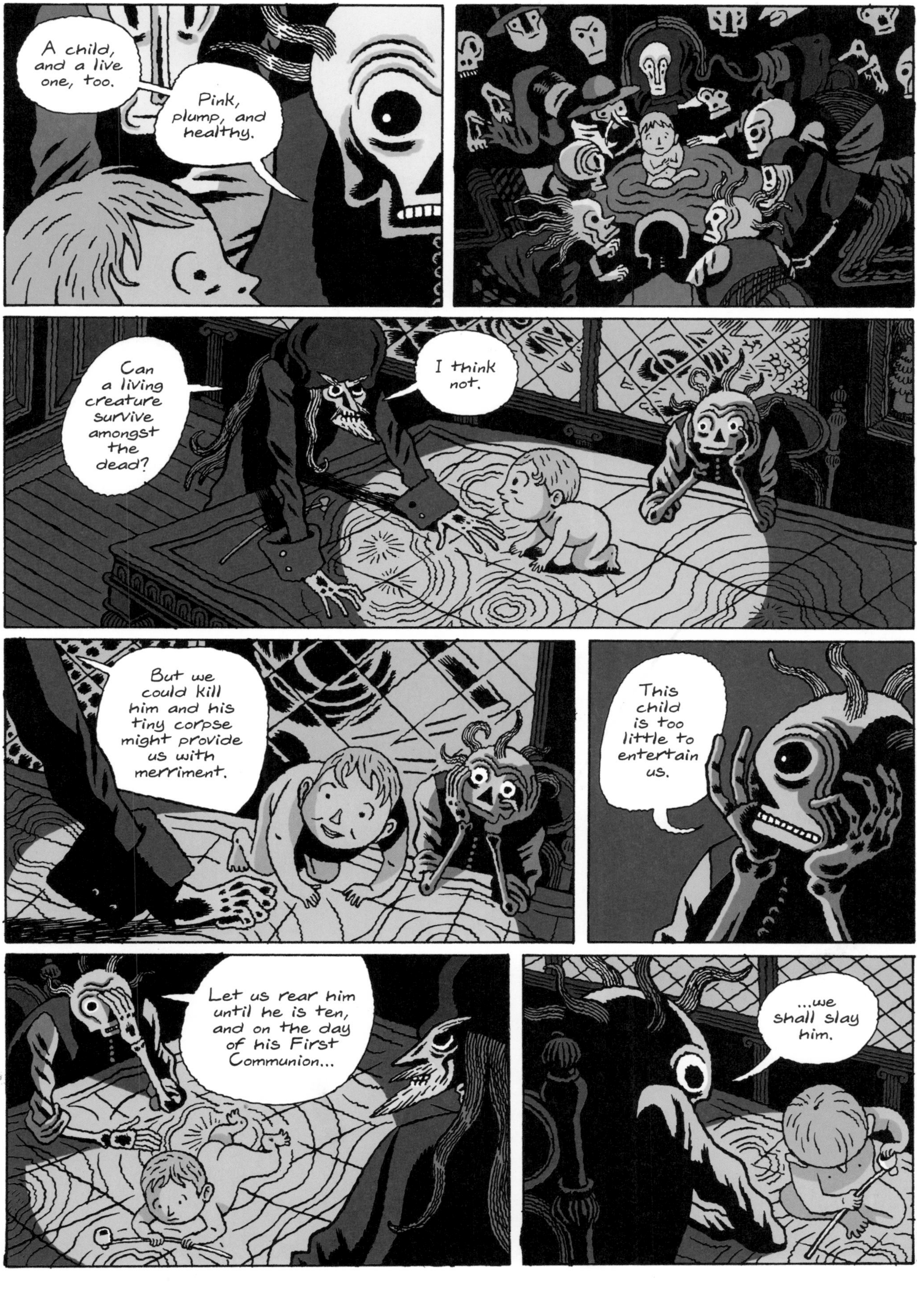
A child, and a live one, too.
Pink, plump, and healthy.
Can a living creature survive amongst the dead?
I think not.
But we could kill him and his tiny corpse might provide us with merriment.
This child is too little to entertain us.
Let us rear him until he is ten, and on the day of his First Communion...
...we shall slay him.

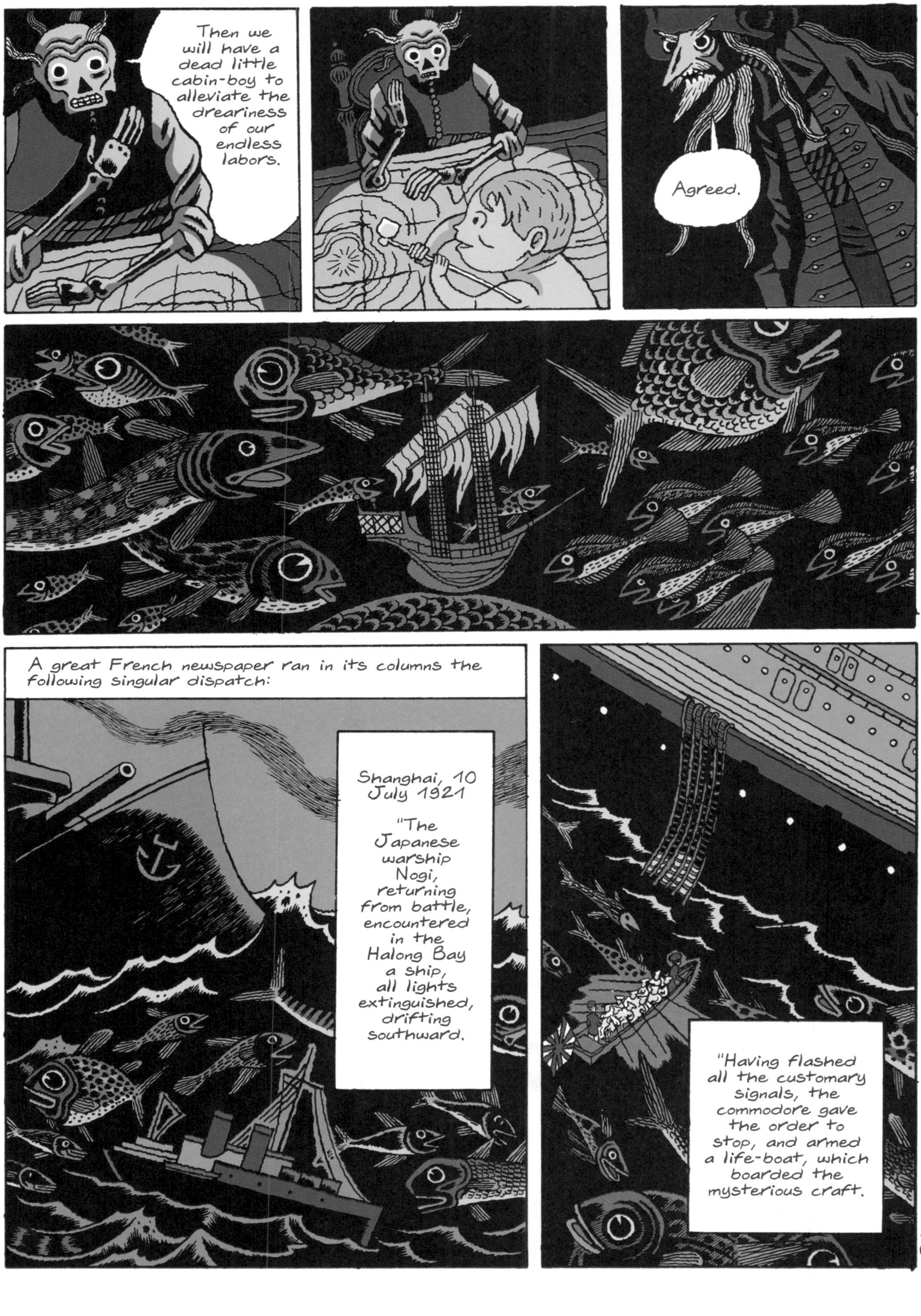

Then we will have a dead little cabin-boy to alleviate the dreariness of our endless labors.
Agreed.
A great French newspaper ran in its columns the following singular dispatch:
Shanghai, 10 July 1921
"The Japanese warship Nogi, returning from battle, encountered in the Halong Bay a ship, all lights extinguished, drifting southward.
"Having flashed all the customary signals, the commodore gave the order to stop, and armed a life-boat, which boarded the mysterious craft.

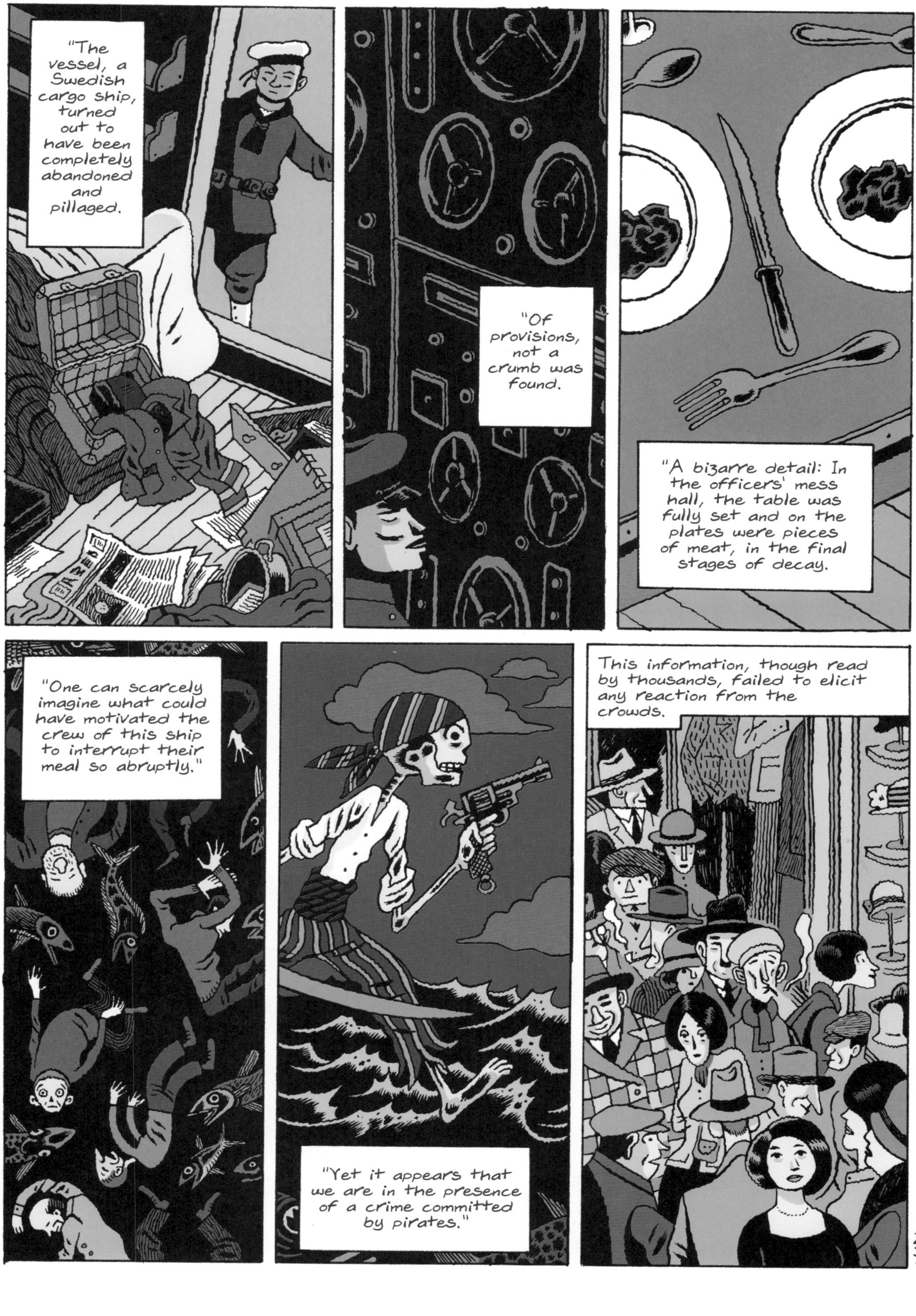
"The vessel, a Swedish cargo ship, turned out to have been completely abandoned and pillaged.
"Of provisions, not a crumb was found.
"A bizarre detail: In the officers' mess hall, the table was fully set and on the plates were pieces of meat, in the final stages of decay.
"One can scarcely imagine what could have motivated the crew of this ship to interrupt their meal so abruptly."
"Yet it appears that we are in the presence of a crime committed by pirates."
This information, though read by thousands, failed to elicit any reaction from the crowds.

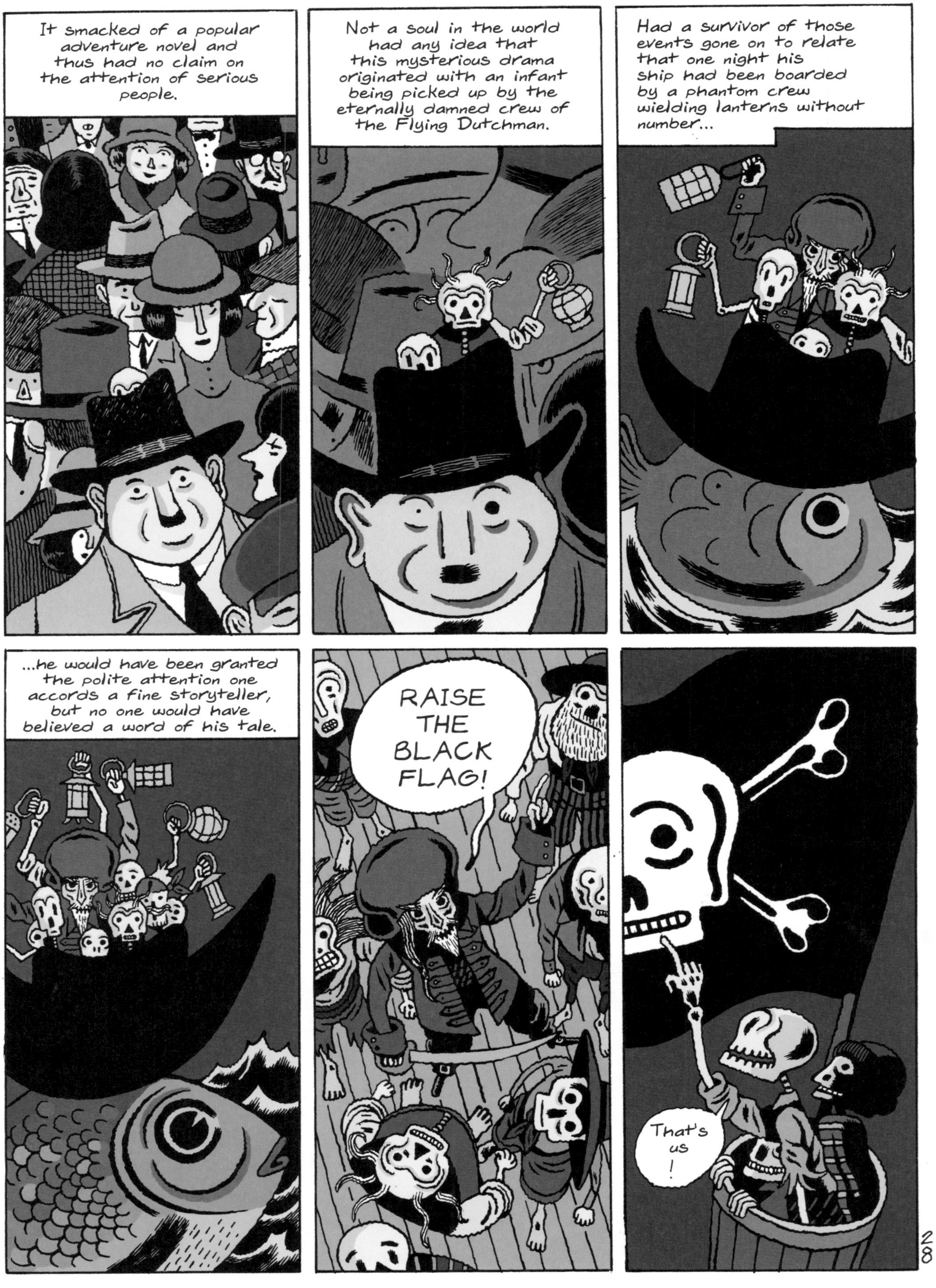
It smacked of a popular adventure novel and thus had no claim on the attention of serious people.
Not a soul in the world had any idea that this mysterious drama originated with an infant being picked up by the eternally damned crew of the Flying Dutchman.
Had a survivor of those events gone on to relate that one night his ship had been boarded by a phantom crew wielding lanterns without number...
...he would have been granted the polite attention one accords a fine storyteller, but no one would have believed a word of his tale.
RAISE THE BLACK FLAG!
That's us!

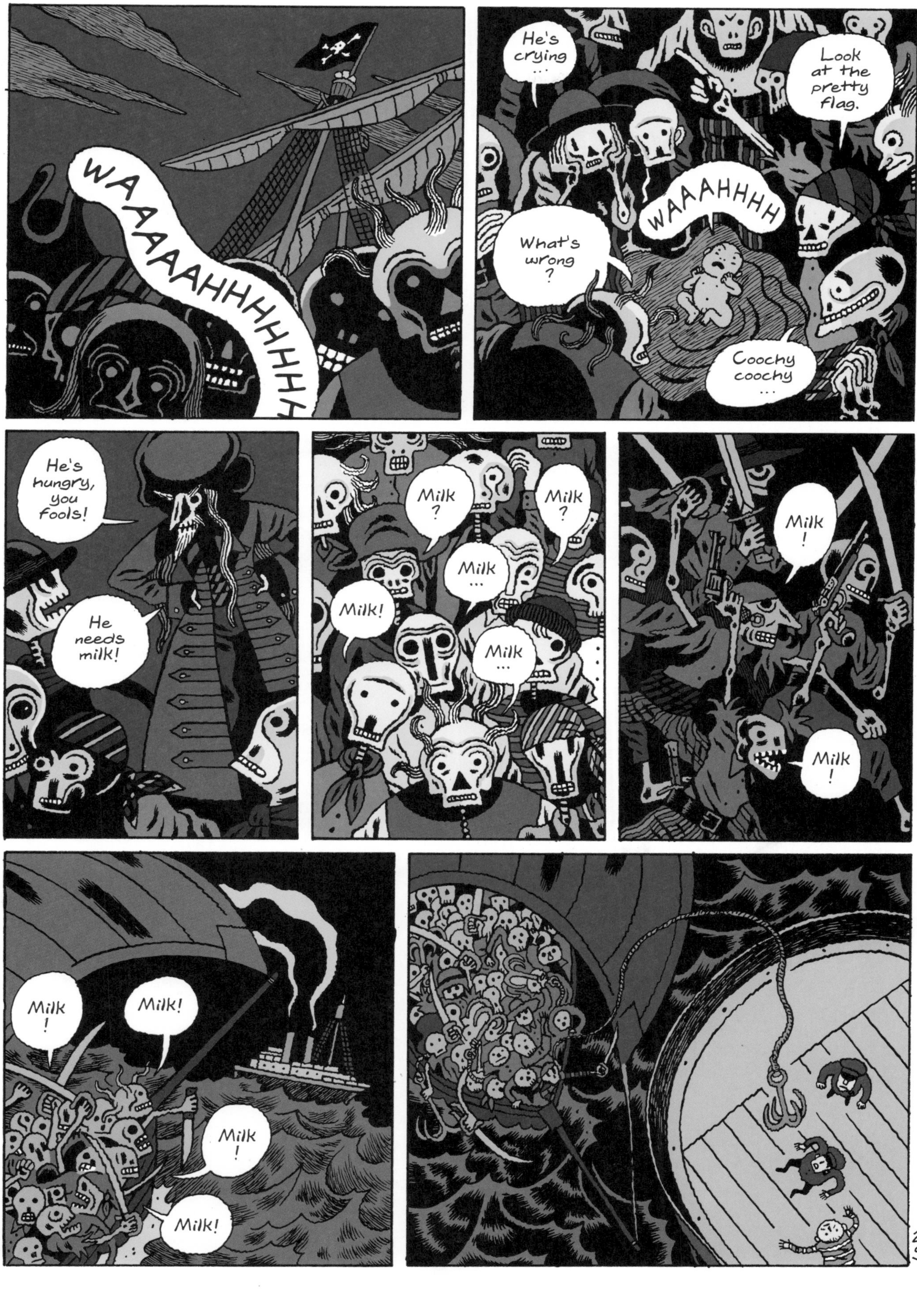
WAAAAAHHHHHHH
He's crying...
Look at the pretty flag.
WAAAHHHH
What's wrong?
Coochy coochy...
He's hungry, you fools!
He needs milk!
Milk?
Milk?
Milk...
Milk!
Milk...
Milk!
Milk!
Milk!
Milk!
Milk!
Milk!

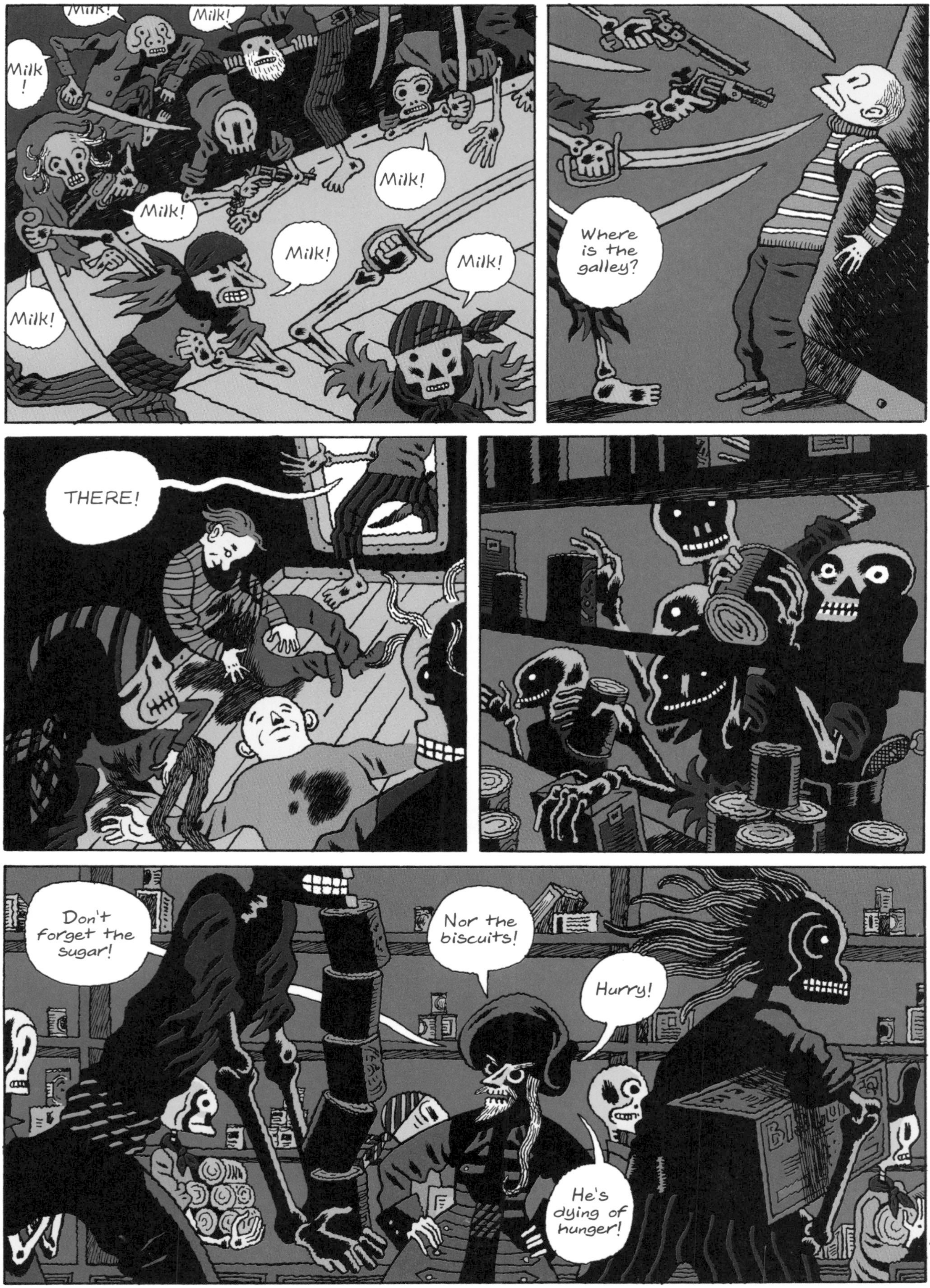
Milk!
Milk!
Milk!
Milk!
Milk!
Milk!
Milk!
Milk!
Where is the galley?
THERE!
Don't forget the sugar!
Nor the biscuits!
Hurry!
He's dying of hunger!

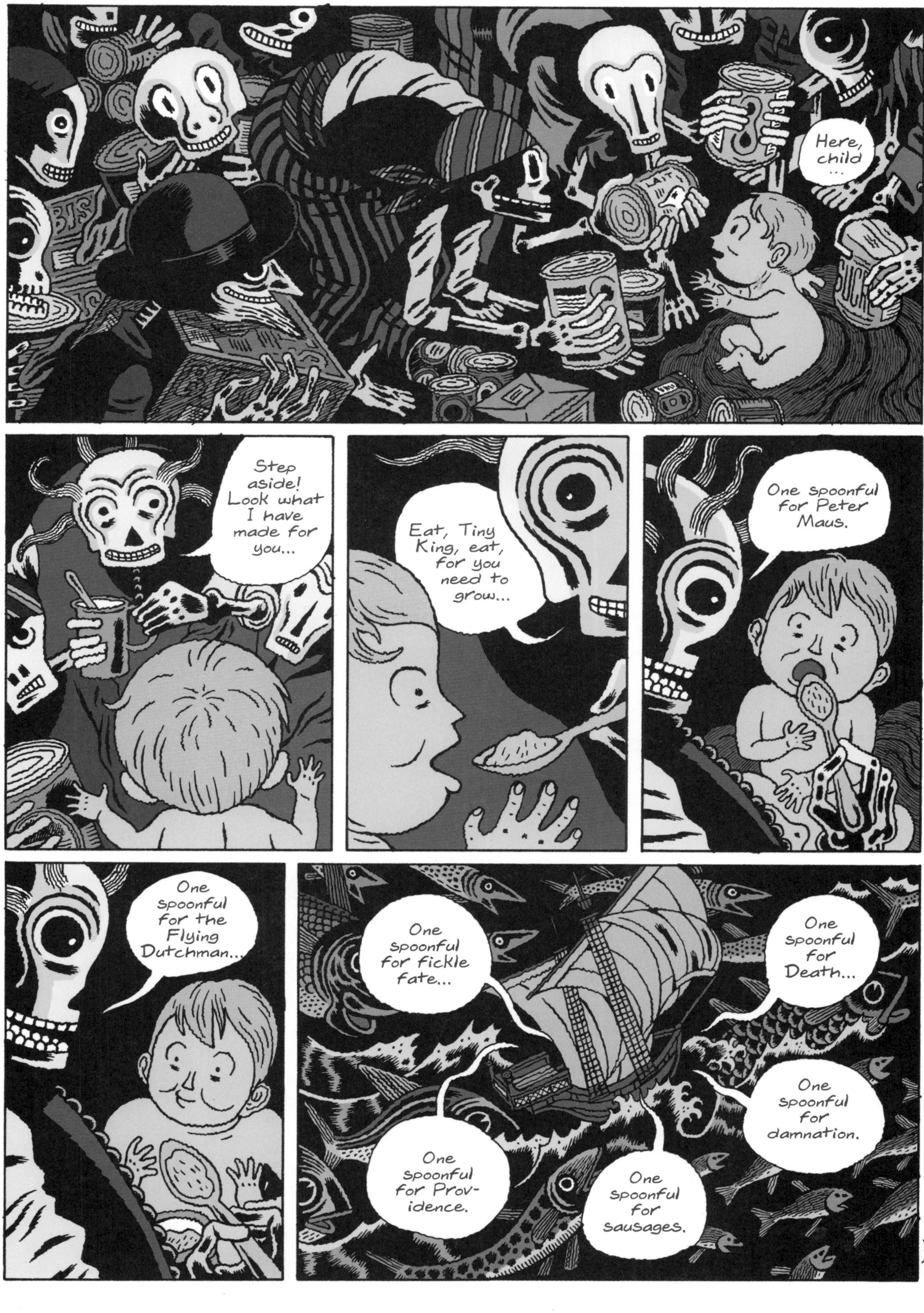
Here, child ...
Step aside! Look what I have made for you...
Eat, Tiny King, eat, for you need to grow...
One spoonful for Peter Maus.
One spoonful for the Flying Dutchman...
One spoonful for fickle fate...
One spoonful for Death...
One spoonful for Providence.
One spoonful for sausages.
One spoonful for damnation.

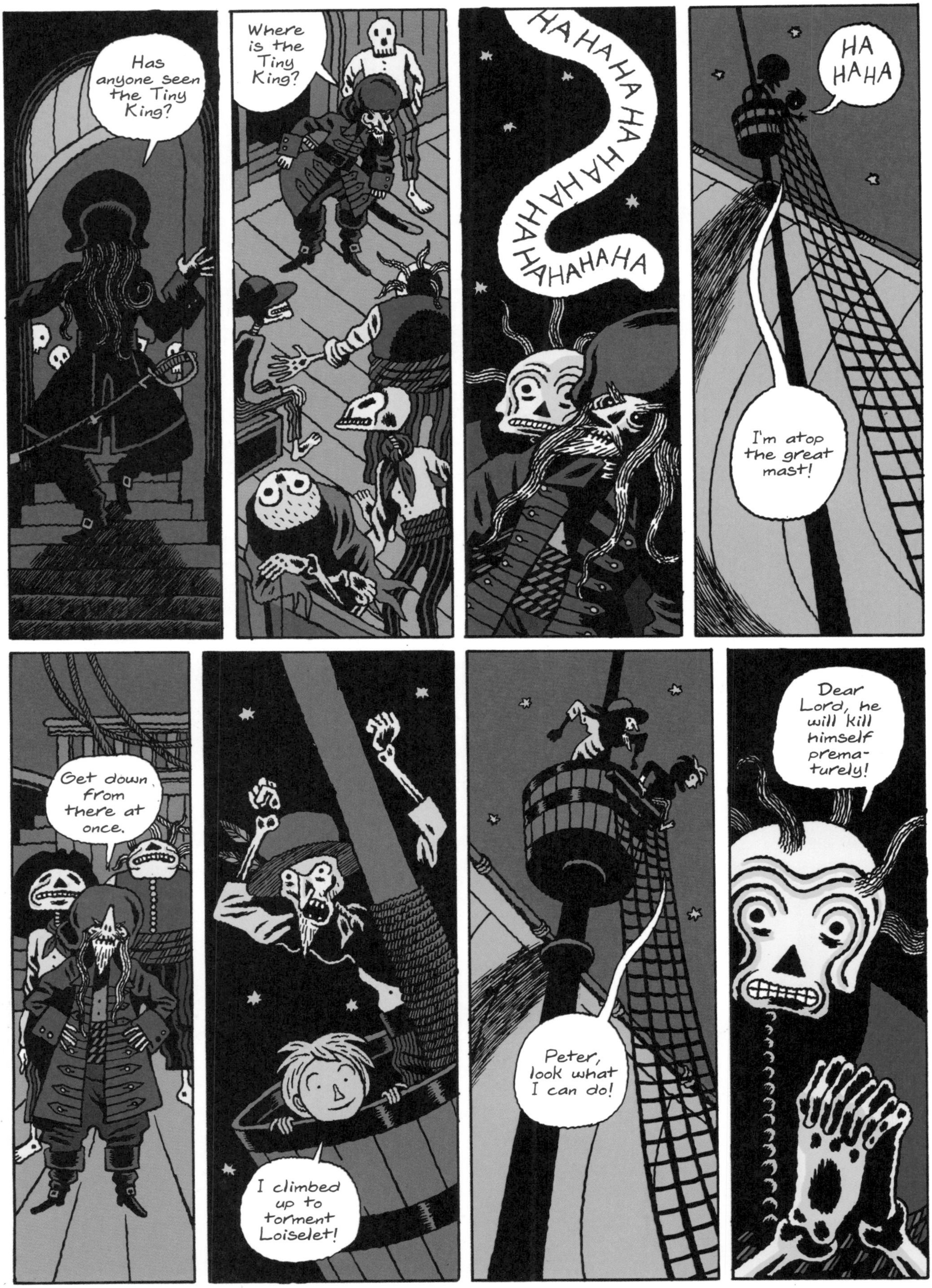
Has anyone seen the Tiny King?
Where is the Tiny King?
HAHAHAHAHAHAHAHAHAHAHAHAHAHAHAHAHAHAHA
HA HAHA
I'm atop the great mast!
Get down from there at once.
I climbed up to torment Loiselet!
Peter, look what I can do!
Dear Lord, he will kill himself prema-turely!

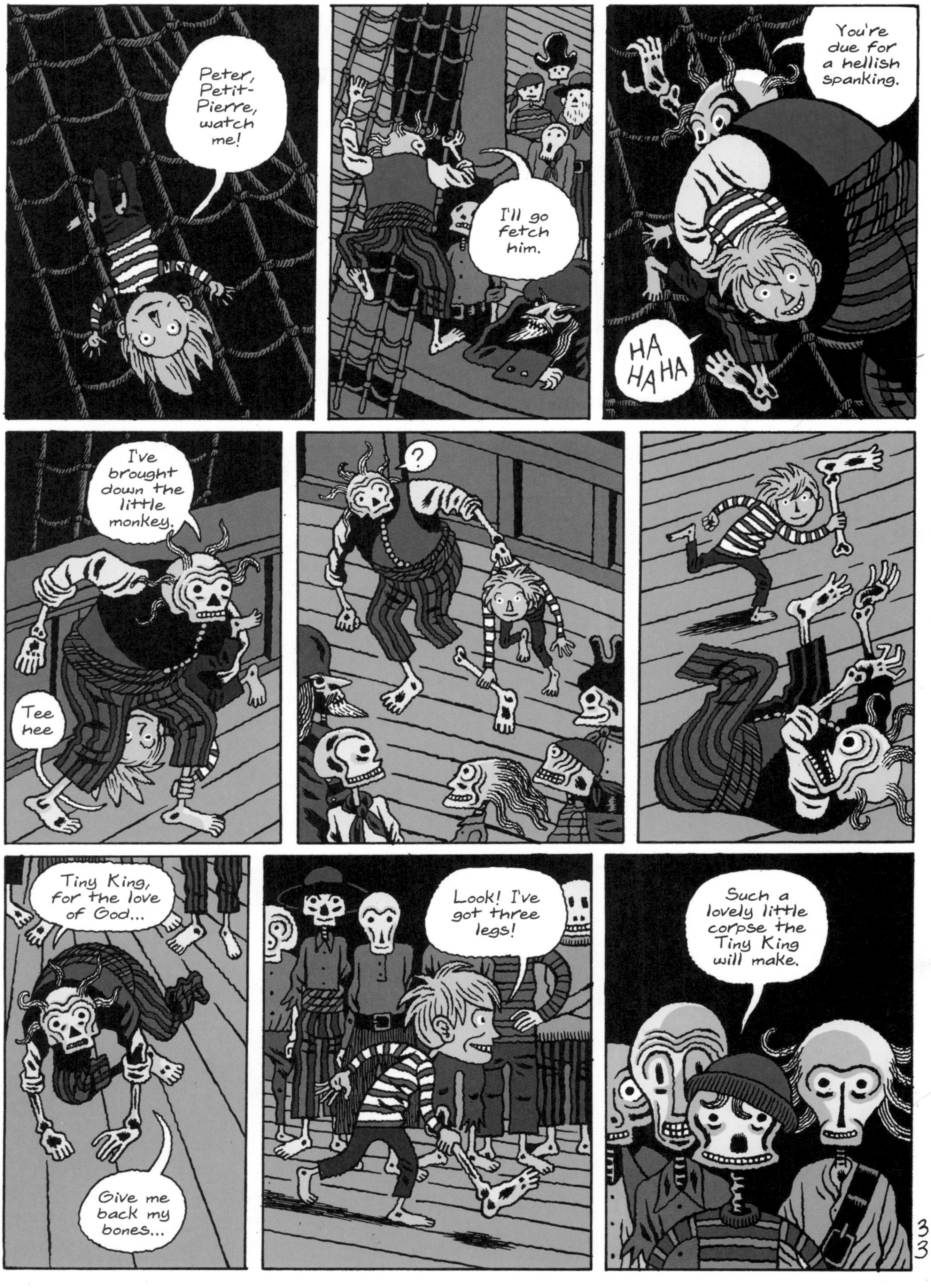
Peter, Petit-Pierre, watch me!
I'll go fetch him.
You're due for a hellish spanking.
HA HA HA
I've brought down the little monkey.
Tee hee
?
Tiny King, for the love of God...
Give me back my bones...
Look! I've got three legs!
Such a lovely little corpse the Tiny King will make.

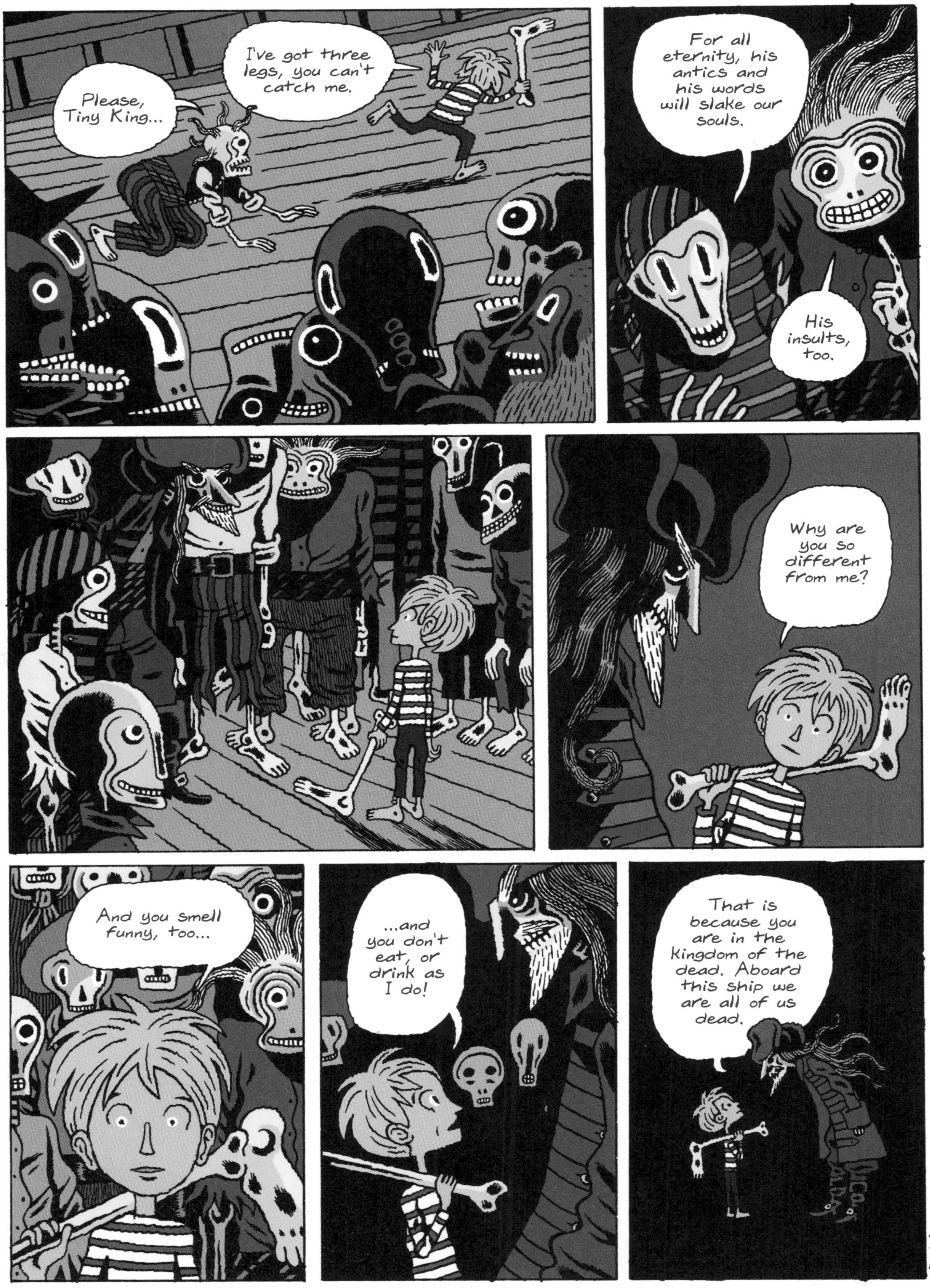

Please, Tiny King...
I've got three legs, you can't catch me.
For all eternity, his antics and his words will slake our souls.
His insults, too.
Why are you so different from me?
And you smell funny, too...
...and you don't eat, or drink as I do!
That is because you are in the kingdom of the dead. Aboard this ship we are all of us dead.

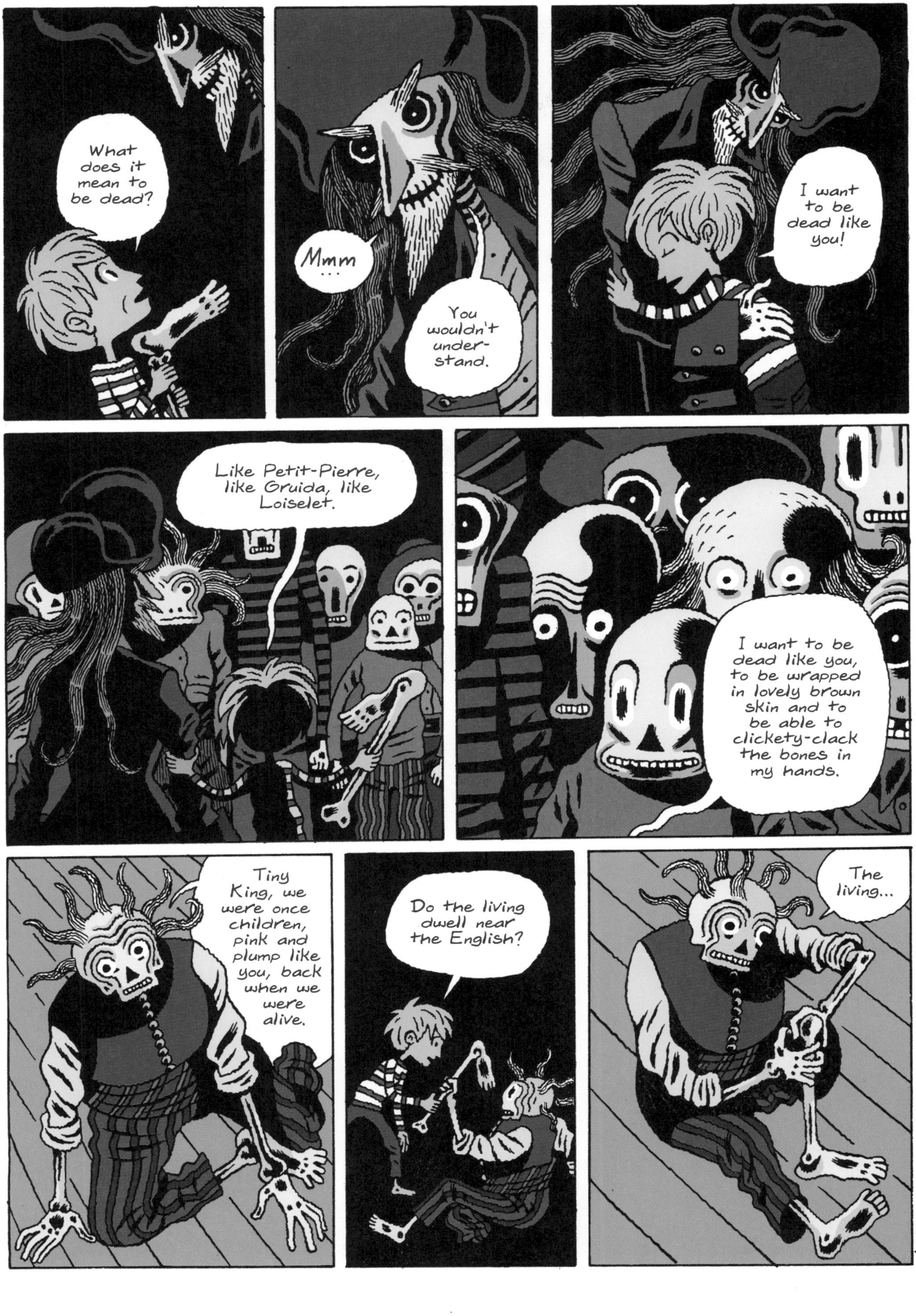
What does it mean to be dead?
Mmm ...
You wouldn't under-stand.
I want to be dead like you!
Like Petit-Pierre, like Gruida, like Loiselet.
I want to be dead like you, to be wrapped in lovely brown skin and to be able to clickety-clack the bones in my hands.
Tiny King, we were once children, pink and plump like you, back when we were alive.
Do the living dwell near the English?
The living...

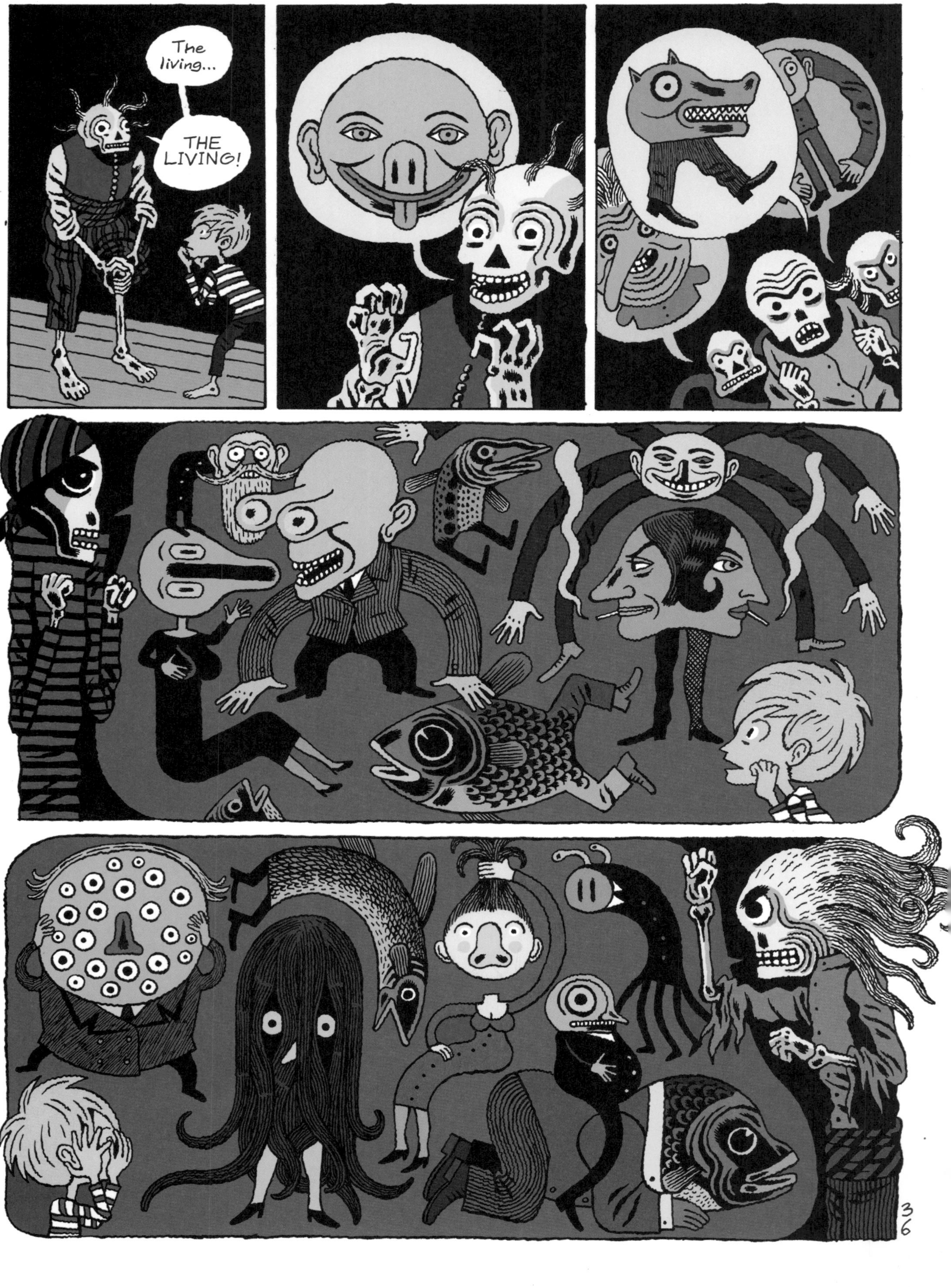
The living...
THE LIVING!

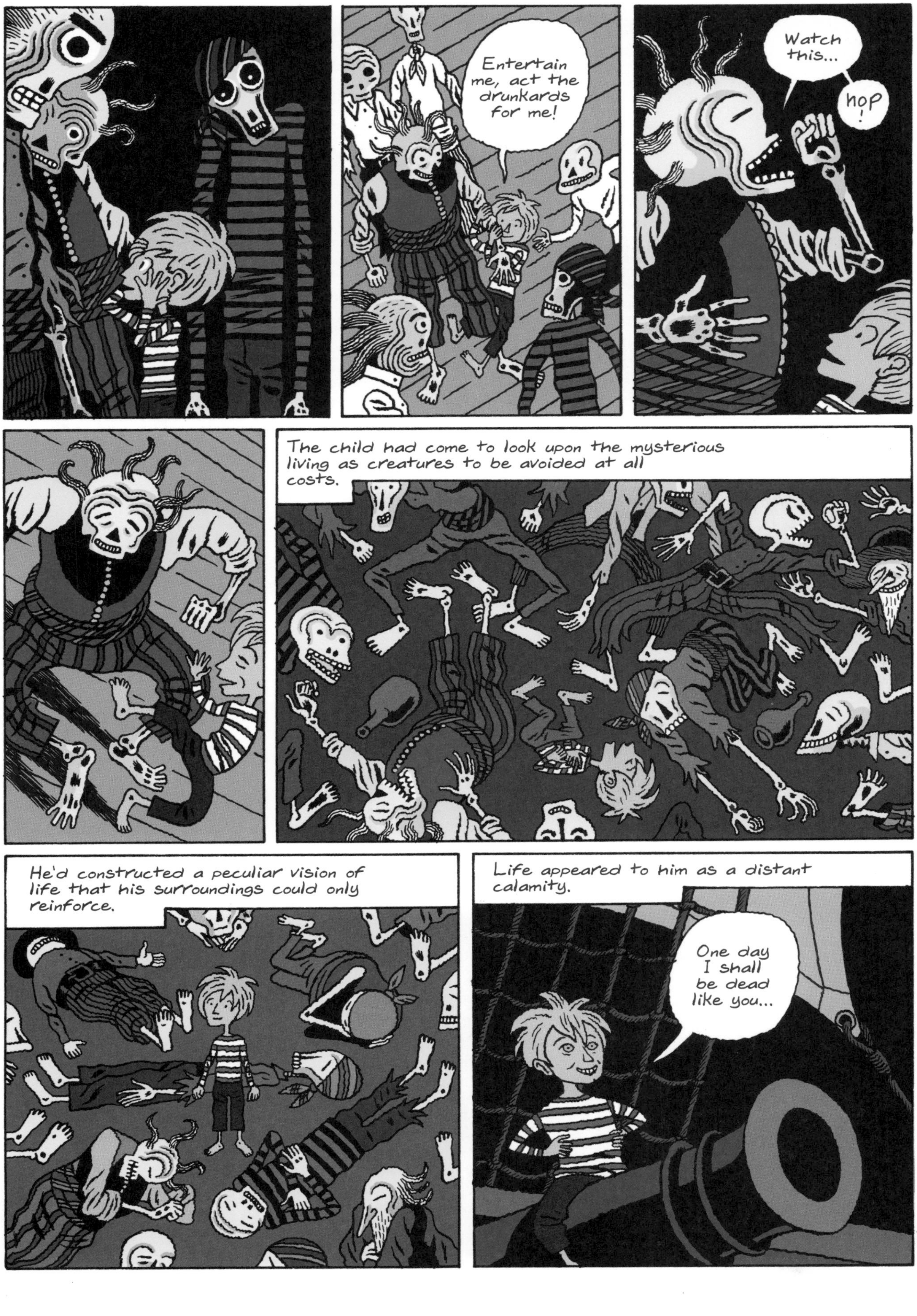
Entertain me, act the drunkards for me!
Watch this...
hop!
The child had come to look upon the mysterious living as creatures to be avoided at all costs.
He'd constructed a peculiar vision of life that his surroundings could only reinforce.
Life appeared to him as a distant calamity.
One day I shall be dead like you...

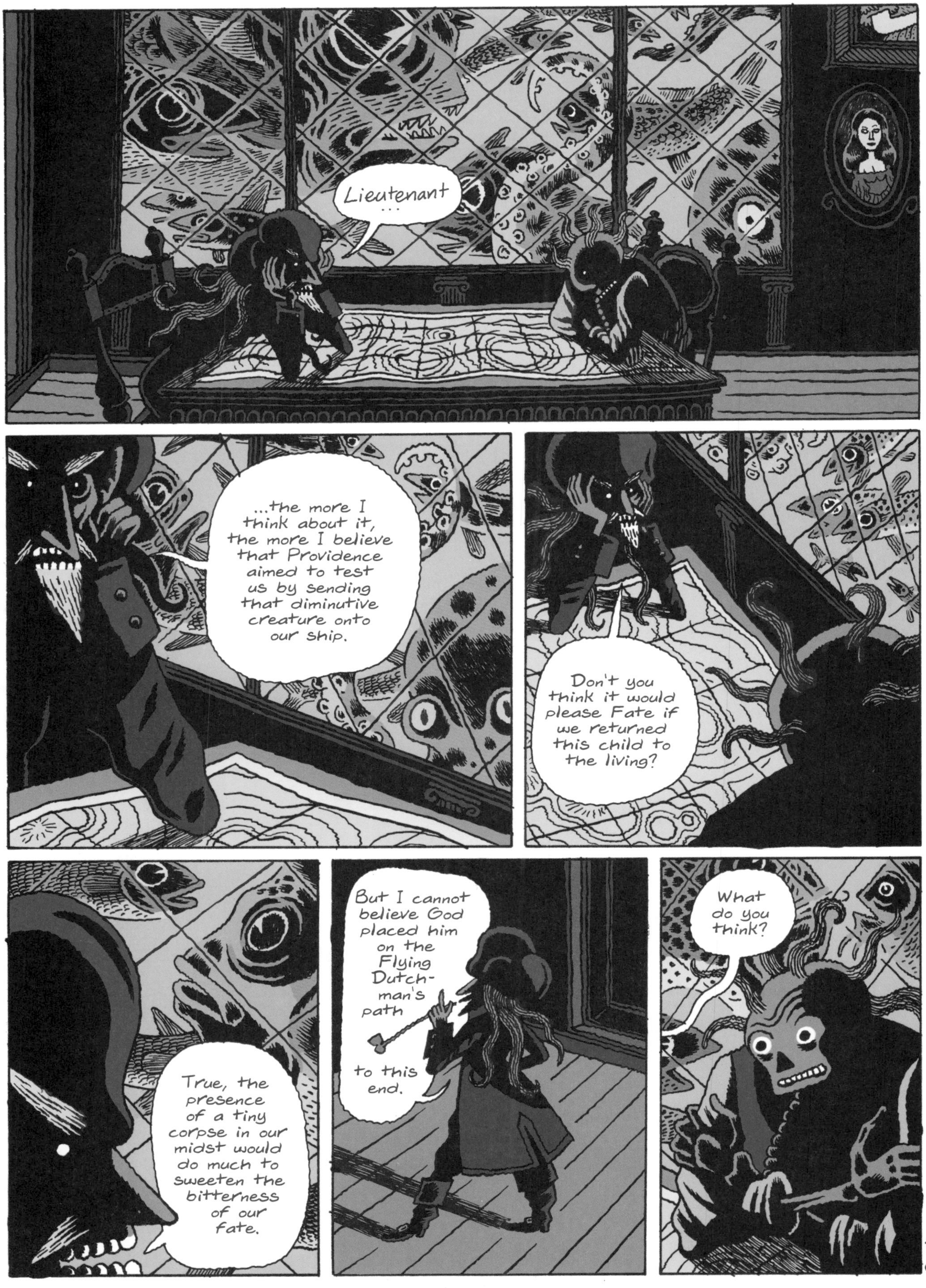
Lieutenant ...
...the more I think about it, the more I believe that Providence aimed to test us by sending that diminutive creature onto our ship.
Don't you think it would please Fate if we returned this child to the living?
True, the presence of a tiny corpse in our midst would do much to sweeten the bitterness of our fate.
But I cannot believe God placed him on the Flying Dutch-man's path
to this end.
What do you think?

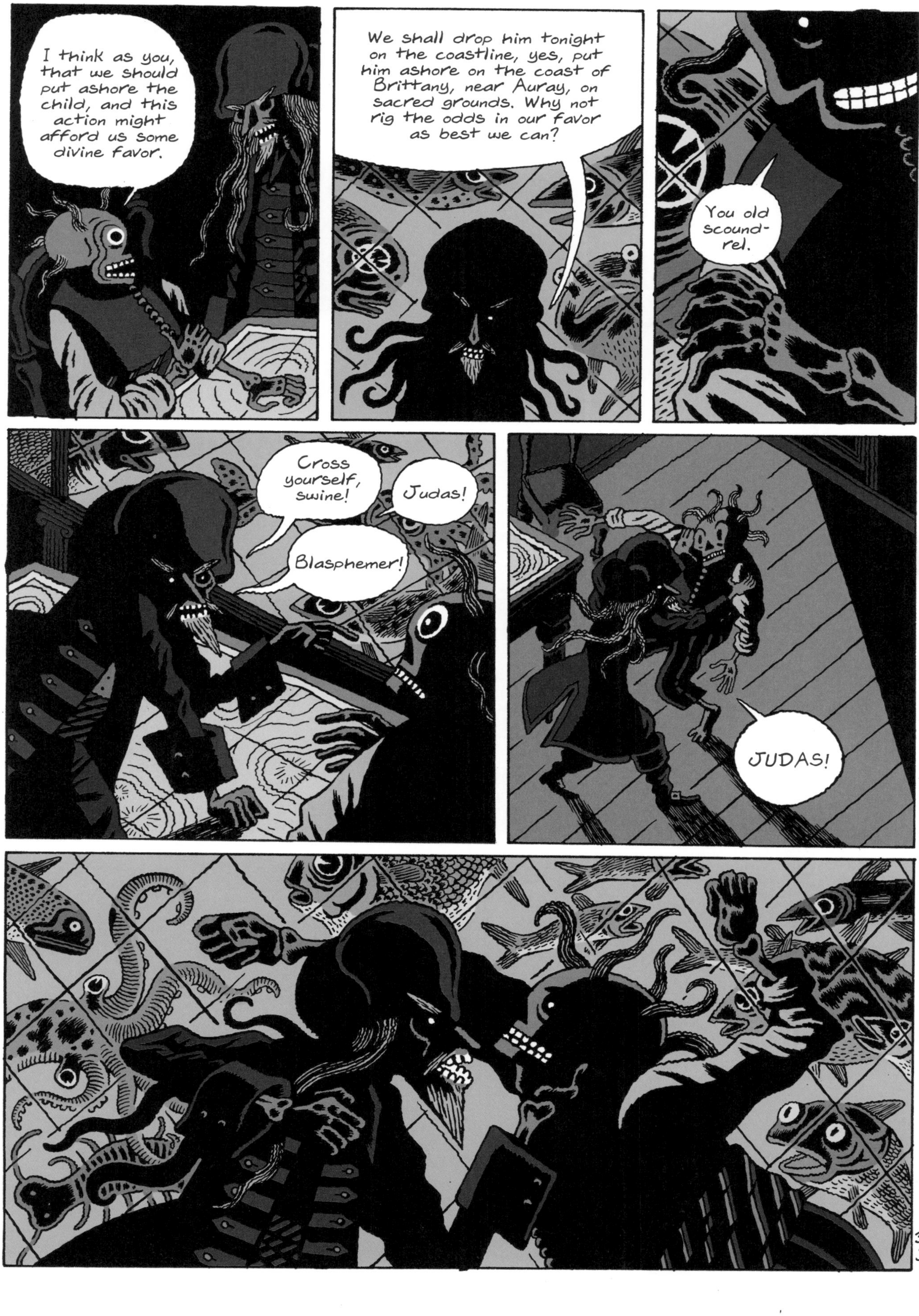

I think as you, that we should put ashore the child, and this action might afford us some divine favor.
We shall drop him tonight on the coastline, yes, put him ashore on the coast of Brittany, near Auray, on sacred grounds. Why not rig the odds in our favor as best we can?
You old scound-rel.
Cross yourself, swine!
Judas!
Blasphemer!
JUDAS!

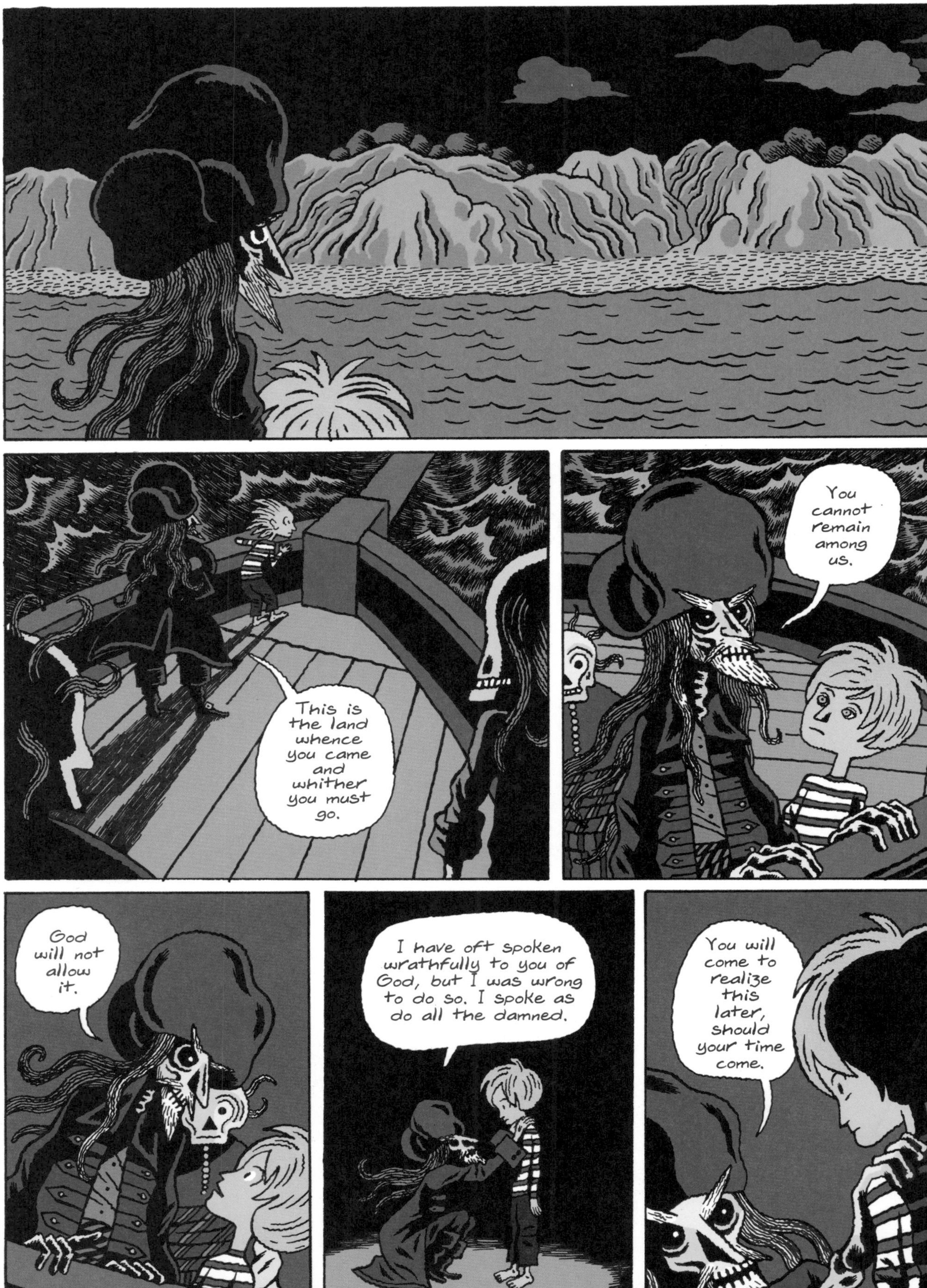
This is the land whence you came and whither you must go.
You cannot remain among us.
God will not allow it.
I have oft spoken wrathfully to you of God, but I was wrong to do so. I spoke as do all the damned.
You will come to realize this later, should your time come.

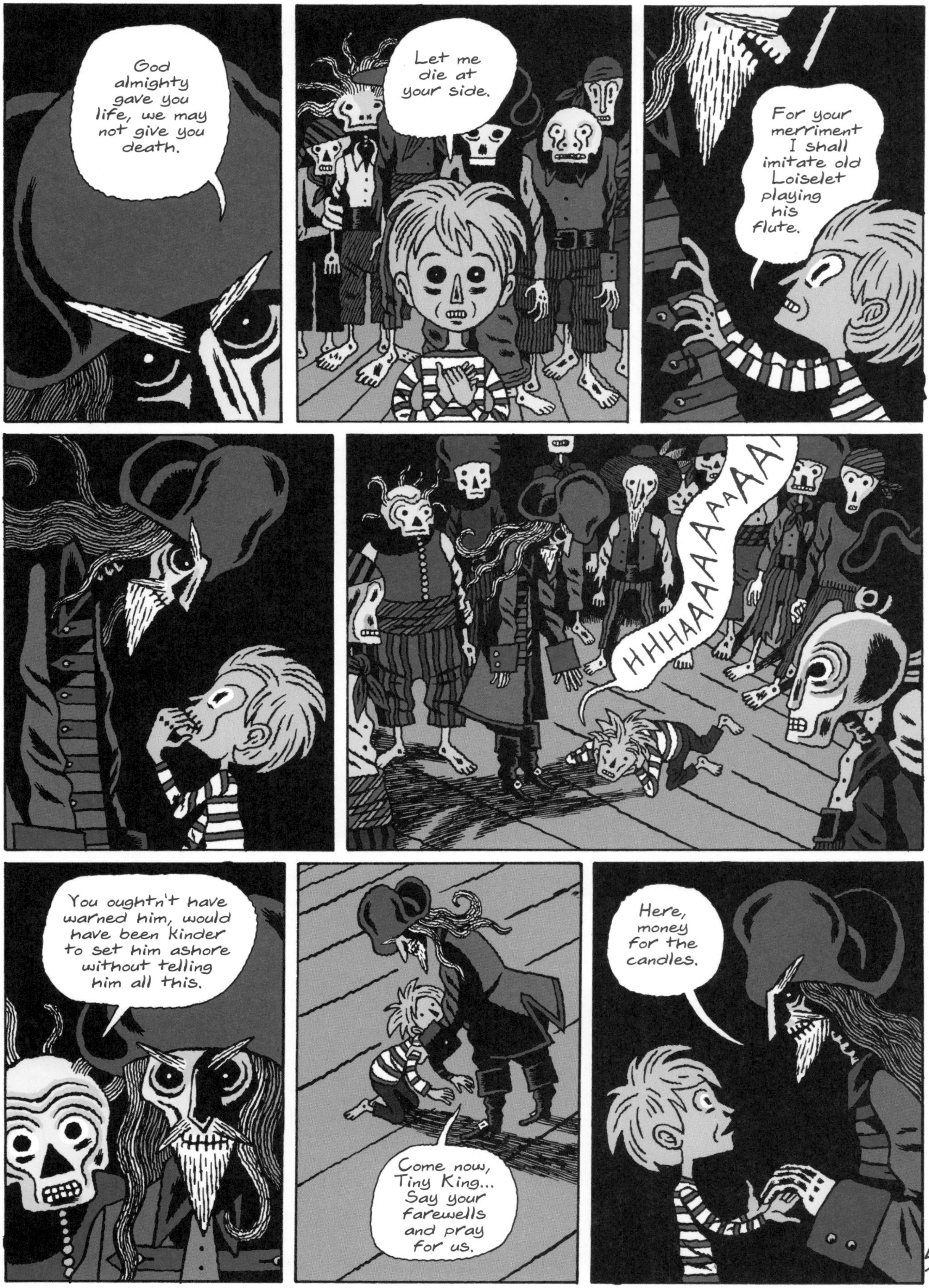
God almighty gave you life, we may not give you death.
Let me die at your side.
For your merriment I shall imitate old Loiselet playing his flute.
HHHAAAAAAaaaAAA
You oughtn't have warned him, would have been kinder to set him ashore without telling him all this.
Come now, Tiny King... Say your farewells and pray for us.
Here, money for the candles.

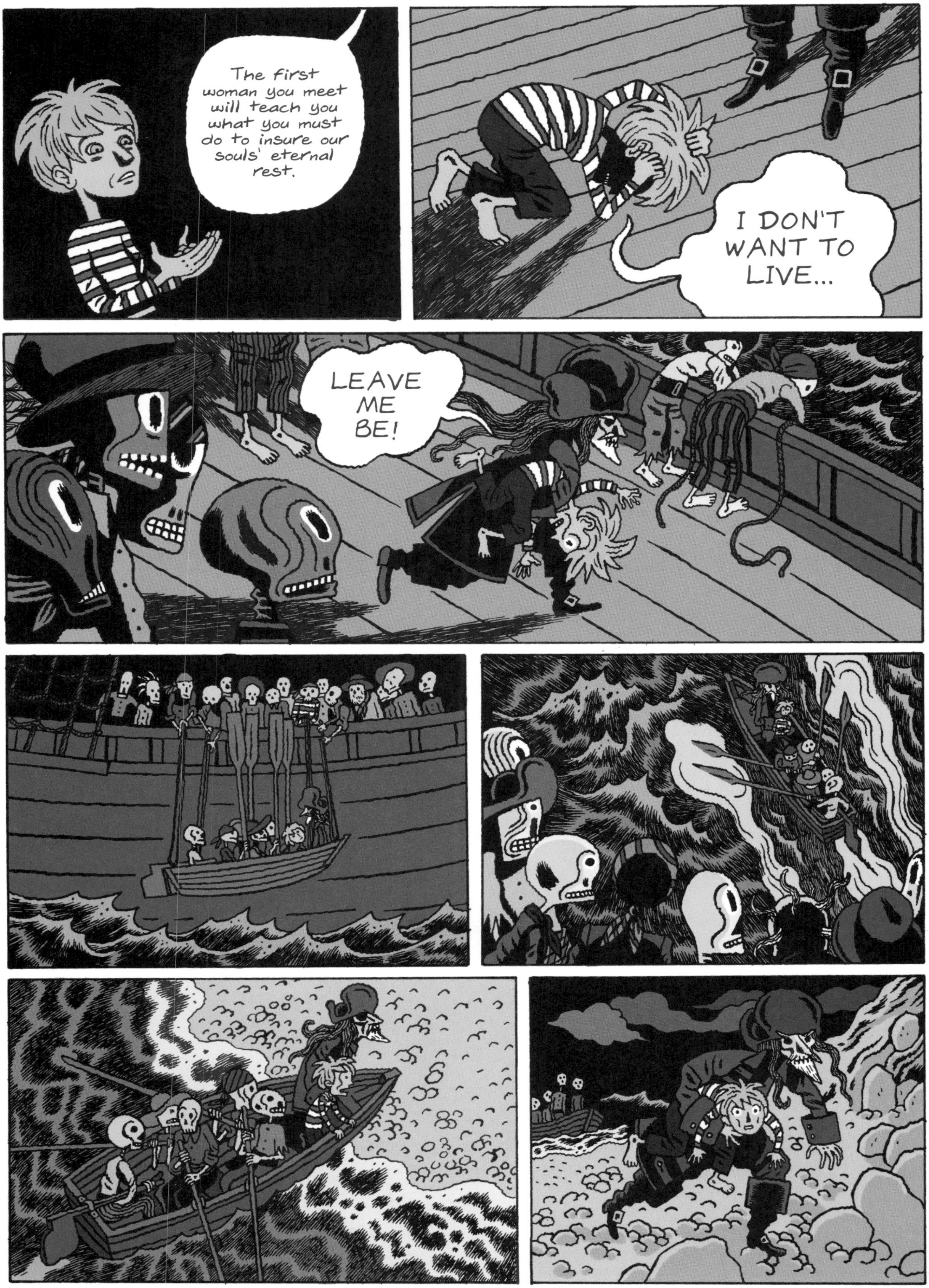
The first woman you meet will teach you what you must do to insure our souls' eternal rest.
I DON'T WANT TO LIVE...
LEAVE ME BE!

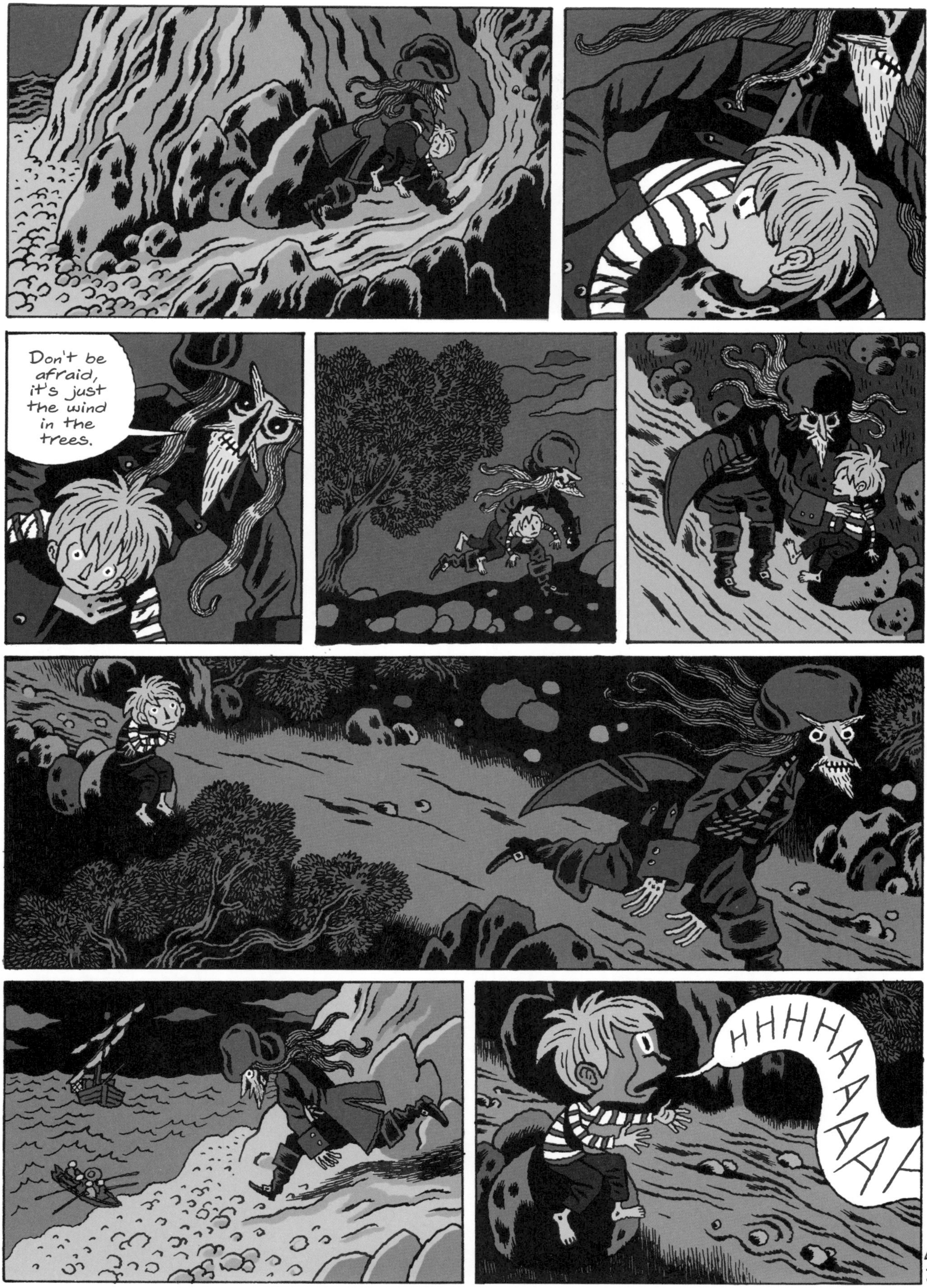
Don't be afraid, it's just the wind in the trees.
HHHHAAAAA

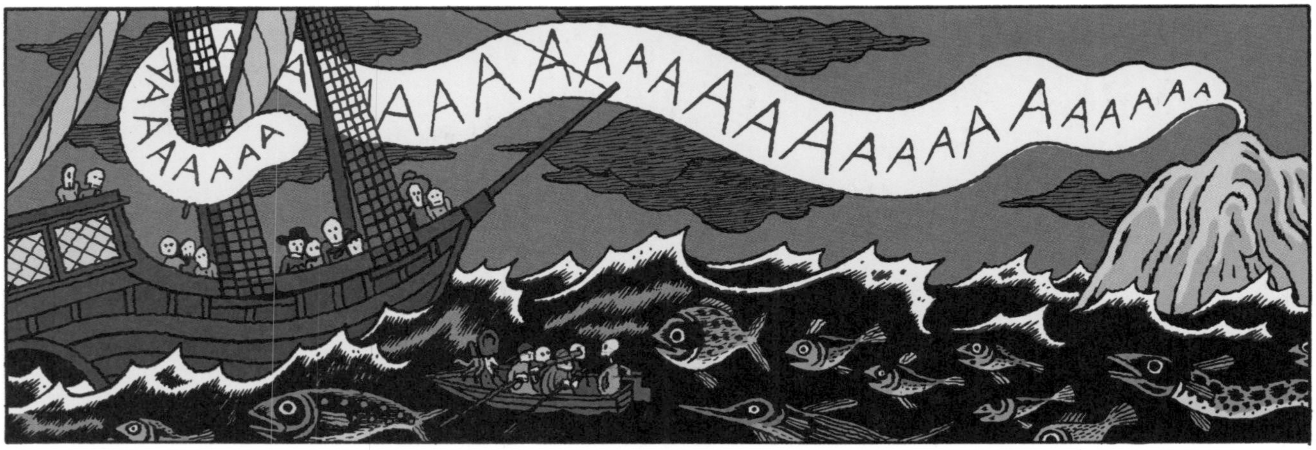
AAAAAAAAAAAAAAAAAAAAAAAAAAAAAAAAAAAA

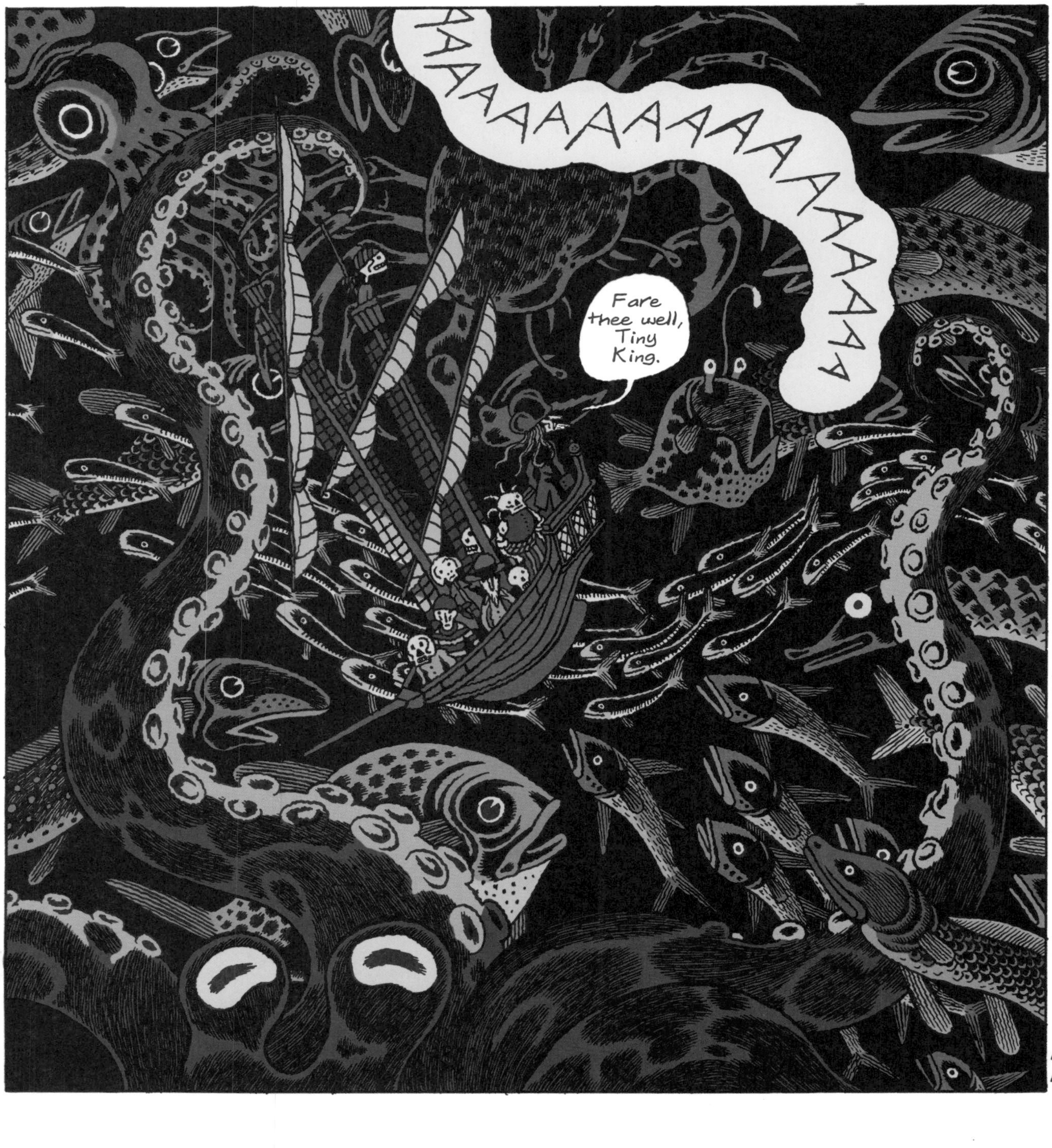
AAAAAAAAAAAAAAAAAAAAAAAAAAAAA
Fare thee well, Tiny King.

A CENTURY OF "BANDE DESSINÉE"

Beginning with the raucous *Les Pieds Nickelés* comic strip created in 1908 by the French cartoonist Louis Forton, French-language comics have brought laughter and thrills to millions upon millions of kids for just over a century now.

La bande dessinée, as they call it, found its uncontested master in 1929 when a young Belgian cartoonist named Georges Remi, inspired by Alain St.-Ogan's popular *Zig et Puce* comic strip (itself in turn inspired by 1920s American comic strips), produced the first installments of *Tintin* for *Le Petit Vingtième*. Thanks to the oddly-coiffed young reporter and his dog Snowy, the man who signed his work Hergé became, within a decade, the most popular cartoonist in Europe (and has remained so ever since).

The 25 years after World War II, from 1945 to 1970, were a true golden age for Franco-Belgian comics, published in such hugely popular weekly magazines as *Spirou*, *Tintin*, and *Pilote*. Standout cartoonists included André Franquin (*Spirou*, *Gaston Lagaffe*), Fred (*Philémon*), Jean Giraud (*Blueberry*), E.P. Jacobs (*Blake and Mortimer*), Raymond Macherot (*Chlorophylle* and *Sibylline*), Jacques Martin (*Alix*), Jean-Claude Mézières (*Valérian*), Morris (*Lucky Luke*), Peyo (*The Smurfs*), Maurice Tillieux (*Gil Jourdan*), Will (*Tif et Tondu*), and Hergé's only true rival, the René Goscinny/ Albert Uderzo team behind the monster hit *Astérix*. And while that golden age is now a receding dot in our rear-view mirror, to this day marvelous new work continues to be created and released by cartoonists young and old.

Many of these great comics have been released in English-language editions by such publishers as NBM, Cinebook, and Little, Brown and Company — but others remain elusive, buried treasures to the American public. We here at Fantagraphics have brought out our finest picks and shovels to unearth some of our favorites.

Our journey into the world of *la bande dessinée* begins with two recent masterpieces by French cartoonists who usually create darker, more adult work: David B. (of *Epileptic* fame), who brings a classic story by the French novelist and songwriter Pierre Mac Orlan, *The Littlest Pirate King*, to sumptuous visual life — while the provocative underground cartoonist Stéphane Blanquet takes us for a visit to the *Toys in the Basement*. Next year will see releases by two Belgian grandmasters whose work has never before been translated into English. *À bientôt!* ("See you soon.")

—Kim Thompson, editor

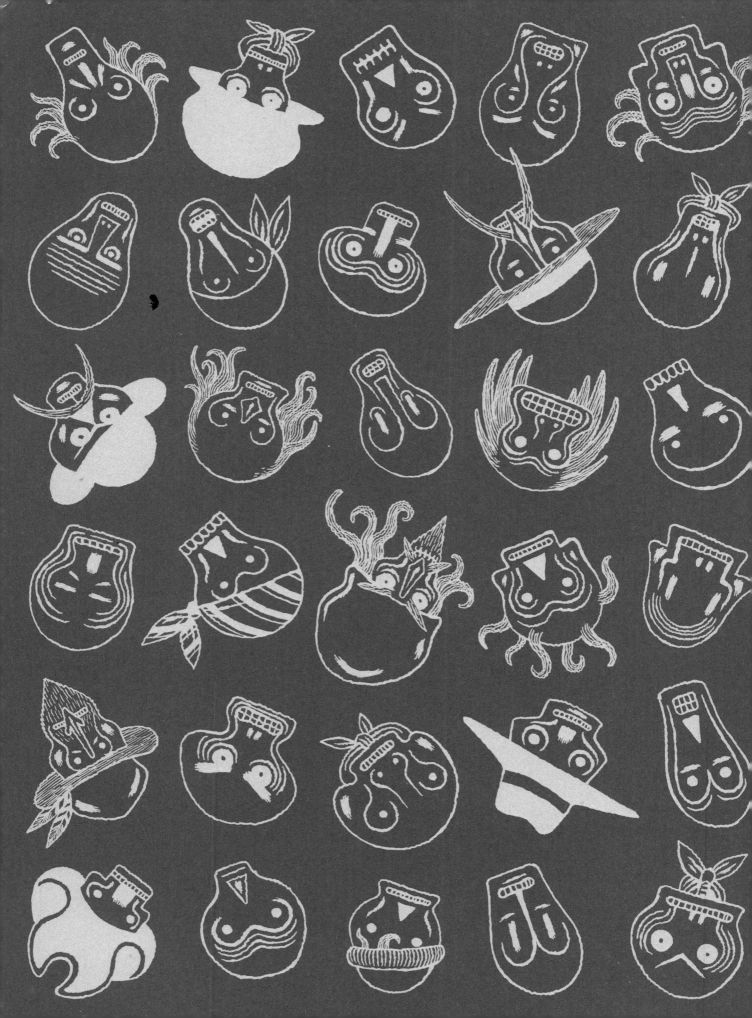